artism

a modern tragimystery

by michael sandels

artism by Michael Sandels

© 2019 Michael Sandels
First paperback edition November, 2019

All rights reserved. No portion of this book may be reproduced in any form without permission from the publisher, except as permitted by U.S. copyright law. For permissions contact:
mcsandels@yahoo.com

This is a work of fiction. Names, characters, places, and incidents either are the products of the author's imagination or are used fictitiously. Any resemblance to actual persons, living or dead, businesses, companies, events, or locales is entirely coincidental.

Please check out my other novels, all available on Amazon, Kindle, and brick and mortar stores:

The End of the Word as We Know It

Extra Special Sauce

2036: The Year Trump Stepped Down; A Horrifying, Factual Account Sent Back in Time (Through Three Black Holes) To Some Random Hack Writer

Two Thumbs Sticking Up!

The Water Salesman

Plays:

"11 O'Clock, Saturday"

"Burning Truth"

Children's book: "The Magical, Grown-Up ABC Phone Book"

Please send any questions to m.me/MSandels

Please Visit the Author's Page: fb.me/MSandels

For Jordan

ACT I

Out, out, brief candle!
*   Life's but a walking shadow, a poor player*
That struts and frets his hour upon the stage
And then is heard no more: it is a tale
Told by an idiot, full of sound and fury,
Signifying nothing.

From William Shakespeare's play, *Macbeth*

CHAPTER 1
(August)

Dutton

It gonna be a good year.

I mean it OK. It just art.

Don't matter where it come from. My brain, my mommy's old brain, my daddy's, my sister's.

Just art. Just garbage.

'Cuz I'm Artistic.

Ha. That funny.

Emma

Right when I saw him, I knew there was something a little off. I couldn't quite put my finger on what it was, and then it came to me. He was too happy. Nobody's that giddy and grinny. Not these days. The world's too cruddy. Yet this guy was just oozing sunshine like he had it all figured out. At first glance, one might have thought he was drunk, beaming while bobbing his body back and forth like he did.

He had the biggest booth at the fair and was selling his artwork for an obscene amount of money compared to the other artists surrounding him. Could I be reading those price tags right? Over a thousand dollars? Wow.

I had to get closer to check him out.

"Hi!" I said.

"Herro," he answered without looking at me. *Hm. Drunk or "special"? I wasn't sure, but I was leaning towards the latter.*

"I'm Emma."

"I'm Dutton."

"Dutton? Like D-U-T-T-O-N? Dutton?" He nodded, still smiling, but never looking me in the eye. "What an interesting name!" I said. "I don't think I've ever heard it before as a first name."

"It a fambily name. Fambily."

"Oh I see. Family." He nodded. "Well, this is some *impressive stuff* you've got here. Really, really *amazing*!" I wasn't lying. His artwork was *stunning*. Unlike anything I'd ever seen. Otherworldly. They were all sculptures, in size ranging from about a foot tall to some that were over four feet high. They were all sort of blobby-shaped, for lack of a better word, all enclosed in some sort of see-through glass-like form, and every one of them made me feel as if I were witnessing some kind of life-altering event, like death, or a wedding, or a tsunami; as if these art pieces were forcing me to encounter wide variations of vast, deeply felt emotions, things both great and terrible. Still, they were truly beautiful, first and foremost, with branch-like, bubbling, encased forms seemingly churning up like exploding suns and reaching out to you. Yet, they were also disturbing; they almost seemed to whisper and beckon to you. To me in particular, it was as if they were saying, "*I am psychologically deeper, and far more intelligent and brilliant than anything you could ever create in your tiny, sad, little life, puny Emma.*"

I really didn't appreciate his art speaking to me in such a personal manner, but he certainly was killing me softly with his sculptures, as it were, because all of it was awe-inspiring; you couldn't argue with a scintilla of what it spoke. And sure enough, just as I thought I'd seen, the prices ranged from $1,000 to upwards of $10,000.

"Wow. Pricey, huh?" I muttered. Dutton burst out laughing.

"Hyuh! Yeah, I pricing it high! It go high more when I die! Hyuh!"

I had already noticed a fat policeman (who was around 11,000 years old and dressed in a baggy brown uniform with aviator glasses) patrolling the art fair with the subtlety of Mussolini. That cop now materialized next to Dutton (preceded by his seventy-five-foot stomach), and he barked out a sterling silver, classic Minnesota accent through his chewing gum. "Hey, y'alright here, Dutton?"

"Yes, Mr. Johnson."

"Janssen."

"Yah," said Dutton.

Pale Idi Amin eyed me suspiciously through his shades, and then walked away. I smiled at Dutton. "I'm a painter!"

"Ha! Emma a painter!"

"Yes, and I came today to check out the Northfield Art Fair," I said. "Y'know, like how many *artists*, and how much *money* they're charging. All that. Are you really able to sell your sculptures for these prices out here in Minneso—"

At that moment, the Gods interjected, pronouncing in unison, *"Silly, puny Emma, quiet yourself and watch what happens when We bestow the gift of brilliance upon one of you lowly humans,"* because we were then interrupted by three *very* well-dressed people, two men and a woman, who looked as if they were lost (maybe looking for the Minneapolis Convention Center, about an hour north from here, seeking out their meeting on space aerodynamics or something). They definitely had no business at an art fair out in Northfield, Minnesota (population 2,020), a town which boasted a sign as you drove in: *"Northfield, Home of Cows, Colleges and Contentment."* In that order. The lady in the dark blue suit spoke first.

"Excuse me, are you Dutton James?"

Dutton shut his eyes tightly and grinned. "Yes."

"I am Susan Forbes, and we are with the Walker Art Center Endowment. Have you heard about us?" Dutton bobbed and shook his head, "no," but Sue Forbes forged on. "Well, we have been sent here to meet with you, Dutton, because there are a lot of people talking about your art in Minneapolis and Saint Paul, and, frankly, around the whole country! Did you see your write-up in the *Minneapolis Tribune*? How does it feel to be so famous?"

Dutton let out a guffaw so loud it stopped my heart. "Hyah!! It art! It just art!"

The taller man in the shiny, black suit chimed in. "Hello, Mr. James, I'm Prescott Simms and this is William H. Haverford Forrest, from the Walker Art Center Endowment. We've been commissioned to purchase some of your art!" Prescott Simms smiled timidly at Dutton as if he were trying to serve tea to a feral alley cat.

"Hyah!"

"We'd also like to interview you for our upcoming

brochure—"

"Hyah ha! Hyah!"

I was dumbstruck. Fully amazed and jealous and... what's the word? *Schadenfreude*? Is that it? When you're happy for someone's success, but can't help feeling envious because it's not happening to you? Or is it the opposite? Either way, only the Germans could have come up with such a humorless category of emotion. Seriously.

A good-looking, slouchily dressed, brown-haired man (six-foot minimum and sporting an average-to-decent dad bod) had been eavesdropping from the outskirts of this business transaction and was now sidling up to Dutton James' booth, smiling at him. "Hello, Dutton. You got all this covered? Need any help?"

"Hyah! Covered!"

"OK, then. You know where to find me." The man winked at me and walked away.

I had to find out what the hell was going on. So I followed him.

Adam

Seeing Dutton at his booth surrounded by his usual looky-loos was a relatively humdrum sight by now, when it came to these art fairs, but the work he brought today was better than I'd ever seen from him. He was growing exponentially as an artist, and I felt a bit like his overly protective older brother at times like this. Like I should shield him from the poisonous business world of art sales, with all the galleries and agents and whatnot.

But then I thought, *Dutton's always been smarter than he appears. Don't coddle him. He'll probably be fine.* In truth, the urge to shelter Dutton James was a hard habit to break since we both grew up here in Northfield and went to school together. I'd always acted as his quasi-guardian. Proud of it, too. Maybe too proud.

To confess to a secret: Sometimes I've wondered if maybe I did it, just the slightest bit, to enhance my own image and reputation. I had been popular in high school. Quarterback and homecoming king, all that malarkey. But I never wanted to be like the "popular" kids depicted in the movies. Always one-dimensional jerks, cruelly picking on the less fortunate weaklings. Well, I was never that. And there *couldn't possibly exist* in me some dormant, subconscious *need* for the admiring gazes and heartfelt hugs I enjoyed from holding the title of Poor Dutton James' Guardian Angel. Could there be? At least ninety percent of my actions had to be well-intentioned because I'd always had a good heart, sometimes to a fault. I truly, in my soul, hated seeing the peons peed on, and I shed genuine tears when Sara McLachlan's ads appeared on late-night TV, with their myriad, poor, suffering animals. That is just *who I am*. Through and through.

But what percentage of me, just now, actually needed to check up on Dutton, and what was the remaining percentage that only wanted to get a closer look at the pretty, red-haired, artsy-looking chick in her early twenties who was chatting with him?

To be honest, this time it might have been fifty-fifty.

And now she was following me.

I'm not full of myself. At all (anymore). I know very well that I'm almost forty years old. I know the days of pretty girls pursuing me so we can "hook up sometime" are over. Plus, I knew very well why this cute ginger was on my trail. It clearly derived from the obvious confusion and wonder that shaded her pretty, petite visage earlier, revealing to me and the entire town that she previously knew nothing about Dutton James, and therefore would desperately require an answer to the palpable, burning question: "*What the hell?*"

Should I have made it easier on her and turned around? Nah, I made her work for it a little. Soon, I heard her pace quicken. "Excuse me? Sir?" she asked. *Here it comes.* I looked back at her, faux puzzled.

"Hm? Yes?" I asked. (*Here it comes.*)

"Hi," she said, "I just wanted to ask...I mean, *what the hell*?" (I smiled.) "I mean pardon my French, but who is that Dutton James guy, and just, I dunno. What the heck?"

"Yeah. Well put. He's an interesting one, isn't he?"

"Yeah, but I mean, should I know of him? I'm Emma, by the way—"

"Adam."

"OK, Adam, so...who is he?"

"Dutton James," I told her. "Son of the notorious Demon Lady."

Emma stopped in her tracks and completely doubled over as if I had just kicked her in the gut. Then almost immediately, she erected herself, her face now a similar shade as her red, shaggy mane. "No *way*!" she said.

"Way."

"No *way*."

"Yep."

"*No way!!*"

"Yeah!" I laughed. This was fun. She seemed to have no filter for either her words or body language. Kind of refreshing, actually. In this small town of academia.

"Dutton James *is Willow James' son!?*" she asked, flabbergasted.

"You've heard of her, I guess."

"Omigod, *I love her!*"

"Yeah? I knew Willow a little bit," I subtly boasted. "Back in the day."

"Really?"

"Sure," I said. "She never liked me too much, but I think she appreciated me looking after Dutton in school."

Once again, this eccentric Emma girl sort of convulsed, contorted, and then bent down as if she were about to vomit on her shoes, evidently absolutely unable to control her body and/or emotions. (I think I was in love!) Her body shook with silent laughter as she bent over, like a boiling cauldron filled with orangey-red bubbles, floating and popping, and then she stood up, o'erflowing the brim and spilling out a bubbly ocean of questions: "Omigod! You went to *school with him?* And what was *she* like? *Did you ever see her paint?* I didn't know she was from here! Wait! She's from New England!"

"Yeah, they moved here when Willow was in her forties and Dutton was just a baby. Her daughter, Lily was a few years ahead of me in sch—"

"OK, wait," Emma interrupted, "That makes sense! I was just at the Walker Art Center in Minneapolis, and they have a whole floor dedicated to Willow James, and... OK, yeah. That rings a bell. So where did Willow James live? Where was her studio?"

"They lived about a mile down the road, and her studio was in Ripo Lake, a few towns over. Right now, that's where Dutton works. At her old studio."

"OK... *Did you see his talent in school?* I mean, he's like a savant or something, isn't he? He's a fricking genius, isn't he?" She was like some frenzied reporter, asking two follow-up questions before you could answer the first.

"Yeah, well, no, Dutton didn't do much art in school," I recalled, "but then he was, uh, involved in an accident, and it seemed to—I dunno, it changed him or something. He got much, much worse."

"An 'accident'? What do you mean, an 'accident'? I thought he was autistic or, or—"

"Yeah, he is autistic. And then he was hit by a garbage truck our sophomore year in high school, and he was brain-damaged for absolutely certain, but... I don't know. He just suddenly got really into art. It's hard to explain."

"Wow. My mind is really just...officially blown," Emma said, while providing the appropriate hand motions.

"I can really, really tell."

"And it's so weird," she added. "I only came down to check out the summer art fairs, y'know? See if I could sell my paintings here or something."

"Oh, you're an artist?" I asked.

"Well, yeah, but I mean... nothing like *that*," she sort of whined. "I mean, not like what Dutton is doing! It's so good! It makes me feel... I dunno! And then those people just go right up and say, 'Hey, here's a million dollars!' I mean, *how do you even sell stuff for as much as he does?* How do you even sell art, *period*!?

I thought I could try maybe for a hundred bucks here or there with a really good painting, but he makes me feel... I feel like..."

"Salieri?"

"What's that?"

"Salieri," I said. "You ever see *Amadeus*?" Emma looked at me like I had hiccups. "The play, the movie?"

"Omigod! That's it!" she suddenly blurted. "He was the guy who was so jealous of Mozart, right? Like he couldn't believe that God could put that much talent in the body of, of a boy! A silly boy! And Salieri was, like, classically trained and everything—right?—but he didn't have... *it!* He didn't have that spark of genius or, or... Yeah. That's what it feels like. Salieri. Schadenfreude."

"Who's that?"

"No, it's that feeling when you, you—"

"Oh. Yeah." I said. "That German thing?"

"Yes! It's like you *can't help* feeling depressed or angry at yourself because you can't... *create what Dutton can*, frankly!"

"Well, that's the definition of 'jealousy,' isn't it? A mixture of sadness and anger?"

"Yeah, huh? I guess so."

I frowned at a sudden thought. "Wait a minute. I think it's the opposite. I think *schadenfreude* is when you're privately happy at someone's misfortune. Because in German, *schadenfreude* means 'harm-joy.'"

"Omigod," Emma said, "That's even more German!"

"I think what you're thinking of is actually the opposite of *schadenfreude*. And, no kidding, I think it's called '*freudenschade*.' It's reversed, see? So now it means "joy-harm." It's more like envy."

Emma looked as if she wasn't sure if I was joking or not. (I wasn't.) "OK... I mean, you're right, I guess. It's all just jealousy," she agreed, and then paused for a second. At this point, that was a bit of a shocker. I surmised her dyspeptic, boiling cauldron was almost fully drained. Then the fireball-Emma frowned. "But I don't feel *jealous* of him! Of Dutton James! It's so amazing that he can just function, let alone do all that!"

"Yeah, it looks like things are going well for him," I said. "Dozens of articles in the papers. All raves. His dad is his manager."

A pregnant pause. (Phew! I felt somewhat exhausted, talking to her!) All at once her mood shifted, and she looked at me, seemingly for the first time. "So, what do you do? Are you an artist too?"

"No. I work at Carleton College," I said. "In administration."

"Oh, is Carleton here too? That's a *good school*!"

"Yeah it is. And there's another college in this town too. Saint Olaf. They're kind of rivals."

She nodded at me over and over, as if summing me up, and discovering for the first time what a boring dude I was when compared to all these other Northfield treasures she was discovering. Finally, she asked, "Listen, you want to grab lunch or something? Are you hungry or...?"

Wow. Didn't expect that. Then again, what's wrong with gaining reward for helping a fiery-haired damsel with a burning need of information?

"Sure," I said. "We could go to Froggy Bottoms River Pub and Lily PADio. They've got sandwiches and stuff."

"Great! Cool! Let's do it!"

"Alrighty then! Froggy Bottoms River Pub and Lily PADio it is!"

As we walked together, Emma asked, "Is there a shorter nickname for Froggy Bottoms Riv—?"

"Absolutely not," I said as we walked.

Thank you, Dutton and Willow James.

Sheriff Janssen

"Geez," the sheriff mused. "Just flippin'-dippin' geez. There they go. Just as sure as the sun gonna set in the west, there they go together." Sheriff Julius Janssen shook his head and clucked his tongue. "You see that, Janice?"

"Ooh yeah."

"Adam Winters just up and makes off with the first comely bunny that hops along. Boy, things don't change much 'round here, do they?"

"No, they don't."

"I tell ya, that leopard ain't ever gonna change his spots. Doncha know it?"

"Oh, I know it."

"Still say he's why they lost the state championship twenty-odd year ago 'cuz he was out all night, partyin' it up with six or seven of the cheerleaders along with the Krueger boy."

"You've told me."

"Walks into the locker room lookin' three sheets to the wind and smellin' like a Saint Pauli Girl, then goes and throws three interceptions and fumbles three more times..."

"Don't I remember it?"

"Gonna check on the James boy. Some more of these pythons are here, and, whaddayacallem? Those lizards and pythons from the city are here, tryin' to trip him up probably." Sheriff Janssen strolled over to Dutton's booth and folded his arms. "How you doin' over here, Dutton?"

"I good! It just art!"

"*You know* all you gotta *do* is give them suits your father's phone number, doncha? You got his cards here, doncha?" Dutton nodded and held up a stack of business cards.

"Hyuh!"

"Well did you give them a card?"

"Nah!"

The sheriff frowned at Dutton. "Well what the hell!" He grabbed a card out of Dutton's hand and dodged his way through the sculptures toward the trio of elites, calling-out, "Hey, see here, you're gonna wanna talk to the boy's father if you're thinkin' on makin' deals here and so forth."

"I not a boy!" yelled Dutton, glaring at the sheriff.

"No, he certainly is not," declared Susan Forbes, striding over to the sheriff and handing him her card. "Dutton James is an up-and-coming star in the art world, and we only want to help him out."

"Hyuh! 'Star'!" yukked Dutton.

"Well that's all square and dandy. Oh, I see yer with the Walker Art Center! But now you gotta call Dan Auerbach about these things," said the sheriff, "He's the boy's father, and he takes care of all monetary transactions within the James family." The sheriff shoved the business card into her hand. "That's his number."

"Surely, we are allowed to purchase some of these pieces from Dutton today, since that is why he is here—to sell his art, isn't it?" asked Sue Forbes. "We will absolutely pay full price."

"Alright, look, first of all, yes, you can," said the sheriff. "Secondly though, you know he's got the autism, doncha?"

Sue Forbes restrained herself from snickering condescendingly (thank God), and shiny-suited Prescott Simms intervened. "We've exhibited many autistic artists at the Walker Art Center. Stephen Wiltshire or Nadia Chomyn ring a bell?"

"Gilles Trehin, perhaps? Peter Howson?" asked Sue Forbes.

"No, but that type of stuff wouldn't ring much with me anyway," said the sheriff.

"Well, I wouldn't necessarily call it a rage," explained Ms. Forbes, "but autistic artists are a pretty big trend in art these days. They see things in a raw, sort of honest way that others can't. Dutton James is a truly sought-after artist in a very real sense, Sheriff."

"Yeah, well I wouldn't know about any of that," was the extent of what Sheriff Julius Janssen could muster in response to all of that preceding crud. "But, well, I'm just gonna dial his daddy's number on my Samsung, and you can feel free to talk with Dan Auerbach. That's his father..." The sheriff squinted and pawed at his phone. "Just a sec, now, it's ringin'."

Susan Forbes sighed and turned away from the sheriff. "Bill?"

William H. H. Forrest tried very unsuccessfully to smile a Northfield-type smile as he made his way over to the sheriff with his hands clasped behind his back.

Dan Auerbach

From behind his massive, glossy, walnut desk, the Silver Jackal, Dan Auerbach frowned at his buzzing cellphone and laid his iBook down by the computer.

"Sorry, Ben, I gotta take this," he remarked into yet another item of his transmission-device armory, the surviving dinosaur of all communications known affectionately as "the land-line". Evidently, the person on the other end wasn't happy with Dan's *au revoir*, needing to enter into the record one more salient point, forcing Dan to persistently interject his name back at him while lowering his silvery-head down towards the land-line's base: "Ben!... Benny!... Ben!... Benjy!" Flustered, Dan rolled his baby blue contact lenses upwards towards his surgically augmented and botoxed eyelids and hung up the desk phone while lifting his cellphone to his ear. "What's up, Julius?"

The sheriff's usual, huffy Minnesota whine came in loud and clear (Dan wondered if the hick sheriff even knew he didn't need to raise his voice when calling long distance anymore). "Heya-there, Danny, how's it doin!? You in Boston?" hollered the sheriff.

"Yep." Dan switched his cellphone to speaker-plus-camera setting so he could check out his tanning-bed/spray-enhanced tan. Still looking good, for age seventy-eight.

"OK. Listen," said Sheriff Janssen, "We're at the art fair, and Dutton's got some people from the Walker Art Center Foundation or some such, and we figured it'd be a good idea to getcha in on this, yeah?"

"Sure thing. Put 'em on."

"OK, sure thing, here's it go."

Dan rubbed his eyes and gazed out his office's ten-foot-high windows at the Boston Harbor. Why was it always so brown? What ever happened to blue water?

"Hello, this is William H. Haverford Forrest."

"Hi, William H., it's Dan Auerbach. I manage Dutton James' affairs, and I'm also his father. How are you?"

"Fine, fine. We were just purchasing some pieces from Dutton," droned H. H., "and we also wanted to speak to him about meeting with the Fellows of the Walker Art Center."

"Is that right?" asked Dan, unimpressed. "The Walker Art Center? Seems about time I heard from you all... Listen, William, as of now, we are pursuing galleries and auction houses only. Now, I'll have our attorneys get in touch with you if you want to display any of your purchased art pieces from today in any kind of public forum, but right now, we are *not* looking to exhibit in any more museums. The pieces I allow Dutton to sell on his own are very rudimentary and simple, and there's nothing too extravagant at that art fair. Believe me. Rest assured though, it won't be too long before he'll be fetching upwards of hundreds of thousands per piece, so buy whatever you can, while you can, because Dutton's got some big, big things in the works for the Sotheby's auction houses by the end of the year. My attorneys will contact you concerning our fee for the interview with the Fellows, if we even do agree to it, which I doubt. Meanwhile, do not actively negotiate with Dutton James. From here on in, everything goes through our attorneys at McDermott, Will & Emory in Atlanta. Good day."

Dan Auerbach hung up and placed his cell phone face down on the desk. He closed his eyes and listened to the silence, broken only by the monotonous ticking from his glossy, cherrywood grandfather clock. The art dealer widely known as "the Silver Jackal" (not only because of his full head of smoothed-back silver locks and slickly dressed looks, but also for his voracious deal-making abilities) was smelling his prey. It was time.

Minutes passed in silence. Then all of a sudden Dan raised both arms above his head and victoriously pumped his fists in the air. It was time. *Time to cash in. Time to call THE gallery*. The only one that mattered. The gallery that originally put his ex-wife Willow James on the map and made him a damned *fortune*.

The Silver Jackal shook his head, sniffed, and brooded over the considerable years that had passed, and all the deaths, God, so many deaths. All his friends were practically gone.

And death had hardened Dan Auerbach. He would never give his heart to anything again, not really. However, he had also learned long ago that as long as he kept making money, mountains and glaciers of money, as long as he kept achieving that high, then the lows would never even exist.

Maya

Maya Slotky would best be described as exotic-looking (her mother was African American and her father, Russian). A Manhattan gallery owner with a chic, pixie haircut, she reminded many of an older (and meaner) and very highly educated Halle Barry. Maya came supplied with an old soul and a savvy-yet-merciless business mind that evoked Henry Ford. She was also a former two-time national fencing champion in her teens, where she was said to have succeeded *"with inhuman grittiness and an obsessive desire to win, over generally subpar skills."* Maya Slotky had determined she would make the world pay for that slight ever since.

She hung up the phone, smiling, and mused to herself, *Well, that was interesting.*

"Kira, you're not going to believe this," called out Maya. "Guess who that was?"

"I haven't the foggiest."

"Dan Auerbach. The Gouger."

Six-foot-one Kira appeared from the kitchen wearing nothing but a surprised expression. "No."

"His tanning-bedded, papery-fleshed self."

"His skin *is* always so leathered, isn't it?" recalled

Kira Cohn. Also known as Maya Slotky's long-time "companion" and bodyguard, Kira was a tall, Jewish ex-Green Beret whose perks included dishes and orgasms.

"Still," said Maya, lounging on the sofa, "An interesting proposition. Because even if he pulls off his family's usual usury, including refusing to pay his bills, *and* taking his typical seventy percent...I can still see this working out very well for us."

Kira snarled, "What, did he unearth another two dozen Willow James paintings? You know he just stockpiles those things like blood diamonds so he can set the market's price, don't you? Like: 'Sorry, there are no more paintings of Willow's left, so everyone pay double for these last half dozen! Thanks for the money, and *whoops! Here's twenty-five more Willow James paintings that I just found in my garage!*'" Kira scoffed. "Yeah, right..."

"Yes, darling," said Maya, "I know how he works, but no, he's not exploiting any art by Willow James this time. He's peddling some absolutely sensational art produced by their son, Dutton."

"I beg your pardon?"

"To say there's been a buzz about this kid is the understatement of the year," purred Maya.

"Kid?" asked Kira, "Isn't he, like, forty?"

"Close to it. Mentally challenged, autistic, and the son of an art legend. The headlines just write themselves."

"True."

"And his work...it's astonishing."

Kira Cohn tilted her head and gawked at her, taken aback every time Maya was genuinely complimentary about *anything*, because it didn't happen often. "*Really?*" Kira remarked.

"It's unlike anything in this world," insisted Maya. "It's the goddamn future, the past, and right now, rolled into a bunch of sculptures. They are revelatory. And sweetheart, we are being offered all of them, exclusively."

"For when?" asked Kira.

"December."

"I thought we had Henriett Seth F."

"Cancelled," laughed Maya.

"You're cancelling one autistic artist for another?"

"The Autistics are all the rage, Kiki..."

Kira disappeared back into the kitchen. "You know he's lying again, right? Dan the Gouge? And you know he's trying to gouge you straight up the backside, right?"

"That was mostly Dan's second wife who pushed the eighty percent take for them. You know who I mean. Not Willow James. The second one. But Dan seems like he's less full of bullcrap now," claimed Maya. "Plus, this time we're ready for the James family. Anyway, there's certainly fewer of them, compared to years past..." Silence from the kitchen. "Anyway, I'm going to do it. I'll call him back tomorrow and give the green light."

"So he can flunge you straight up your backside."

Maya smiled because Kira was "pricking the sides of her intent," goading her on by using fencing terminology (because she knew it drove her crazy). Maya tried to recall what a "flunge" was. Oh, yes—a combination of a lunge and a fleche with a saber. It had evolved after the FIE modified-saber rule-change in 1992, "to prohibit running attacks." Partially because of young champion Maya Slotky and her out-of-control, vicious assaults upon her trembling opponents.

"Oh, Kira, you must know by now that I've already got him in my rearview, and I am staring carving knives in his immediate direction." Maya chuckled as she clicked through the images of Dutton's sculptures on her laptop. "And that's precisely where I intend to keep him."

CHAPTER 2

Dutton
 I like selling my art.
 So what if Dad don't like me selling. I like to see people and talk to them and have them saying nice things about me.

They lots of money too.
But it just art.
It just art.
Here come more people.
Smile big.

Emma

"Ugh."

My mind was spinning as I slumped down in my Honda Civic.

This isn't weird, right? I kept thinking to myself. *Of course not*, I answered myself back, then on and on like that; critically questioning myself, and then stroking and soothing my doubts until they became nothing but ridiculous notions, usually by relying on the old standard: I'm not actually doing anything technically *illegal*, am I, so what's the big deal? Wow. I'd make a good president.

I peeked up at the art studio across the street. *James Art Studio* read the sign. Obviously, this was the place. Didn't need a GPS to tell me that.

Oh crap, and now another car just came, right as the last two groups were fricking leaving, carrying their plain brown shopping bags, hiding away some small souvenir or art piece from the James Art Studio. Ugh. This meant more waiting. Earlier on, some tween couldn't even get all the way out the front door without having to snap three selfies of herself—holding her shopping bag aloft with the art studio's sign in the background—all the while sporting the frozen, cartoonish, grinning expression that before now was seen only on spokesmodels from 1950s magazine ads ("I just love my new Kenmore!") or on the paralyzed grotesques of victory/defeat that festooned the cardboard covers of board games like *Don't Bug Me!* and *Battleship!* (Ecstatic girl: "I win, I win!" Tragic boy: "Oh nooo!").

OK, I thought, *I'll go in right after these new customers leave, and no more procrastinating, or else I'll be sitting here all day. Maybe I don't even have to talk to Dutton alone! Who says I do? What's the big deal, like there can't be any other people around at all?* I scolded the other Emma, the angel-one.

Still, Demon/Emma shot back, *it'd be easier if we were alone.* I sort of had the feeling I couldn't get Dutton James' full, undivided attention in a crowded, public setting. But if I got him *alone*, I could use my Fargo, North Dakota charm on him: "Say, *did you know* that singer Donna Fargo named herself after my hometown just like John Denver named himself after Denver, Colorado? Her real name was Yvonne Vaughn. And his was Henry John Deutschendorf Jr. *Did you know* that singer, Bobby Vee was from Fargo? He sang that song: 'Rubber ball, I come bouncing back to you, Rubber ball, I come...'" (Jesus, don't say any of that. That's the creepiest crap I ever heard. "Oh, you don't know who they are, Dutton? We don't share an affinity for obscure, mediocre singers from the 1970s, before we were born?" Good God, I was pathetic.)

I looked over again at the art studio. It wasn't on the town's main drag; it was more like one of those sporadic old buildings you'd pass along the way. An old granary surrounded by overgrown grass, then a half a mile of nothing, then the shoddy-looking James Art Studio, then another half mile of very little, and then the tiny town of Ripo Lake, Minnesota. Hey, I was just a regular customer, sitting here alone, on an empty street, at the side of the road, *not a stalker*. At least if I had a credit card I could be a real customer. Or more than $17 cash. And I guess a customer would also park in the art studio's *actual parking lot* since there were seven trillion spaces available.

Still. Wasn't being illegal. I had just as much right to be there as anyone else. "I'm a US citizen!" I said to the rearview mirror, "Maybe not a Minnesota resident, but I live in Fargo, and you can't get closer to Minnesota than that. I pay taxes!" At least I did whenever I bought cups of ramen noodles at the Piggly Wiggly with Grandma's money. ("It's only a loan!" I kept vehemently warning Grandma, pointing my finger threateningly in her face, as if she needed to be scolded for lending me money.)

If a cop questioned for me sitting on the shoulder of the road, I could say I pulled off to make a phone call. Show him my driver's license and my Art Institute of Chicago ID card. Yeah, I graduated over a year ago, but it still showed last year as the date, so it was still "relevant." That would impress upon the policeman I was an intelligent, valued member of society.

"Although who am I kidding? I'm Emma Kincaide, the failed hope of Fargo South High School, along with 11/12ths of the rest of the school's alumni. Living with Grandma. Never sold a damn painting in my life. Could I seriously be more of a stereotype, showing why half the nation hates us millennial, liberal, feckless f-ups?" I asked out loud. "Seriously?"

At this point, unbeknownst to me a tall old man, whose darkly tanned face resembled aged, sloughed-off snakeskin, was standing beside my car.

"Can I help you?" he shouted through my closed window, causing me to jump in my seat while my heart exploded, banging my knee on the bottom of the steering wheel in the process.

"Omigod!-OW!!" I shrieked. I reached down to grab my knee, but then my face bonked into the steering wheel, causing the horn to blare, which then stimulated both of our hearts into further stages of spontaneous coronary thrombosis.

"Damn! You OK, lady?" He crouched his tall frame down to get a better look at me.

"Yeah. Yep." I rolled down my window. "You just startled me. What's up?"

"I was just askin' if I could help you," said the tan man. "We been watchin' you on our cameras for the last half hour. You're on a Native American reservation right now. This whole area is." His accent sounded part clipped Native American, part life-long Minnesotan.

"Really?" I asked, "Does that include that art studio across the street? Because I was just going to go in and buy something, but I was making a phone call first."

Tan tall man stood up and put on a black cowboy hat with a blue, weathered feather in the band. "Oh them?" he said, "Well they's another story."

"Oh? How so?" I asked.

"We granted them an easement many years ago, but that was for Dutton's mother, who supported our tribe."

"Oh. You mean Willow? Willow James?" I asked.

"Yeah, Willow. But she's gone now. Died. And now the rest of her family has been very disrespectful to us. But yeah. We allow them that parcel of property. They pay us for it, so..."

"Dutton is 'disrespectful'? I can't imagine that," I told him.

"Who, Willow's kid? 'Smiles with Fist'? That kid don't understand a damn thing."

"He's not a kid, he's in his late thirties, I believe..."

"Yeah, I know, but he acts like a kid," said the man.

"Well. Seems like he's getting to be pretty rich and famous for a kid," I retorted.

"Is that right? Well, you tell him Littlefeather says, 'hey.' He knows who I am. His father pays his rent, but he needs to remember who owns the land he's on," he said firmly. "Alright, Miss Lady. You can sit here doin' whatever you're doin', I guess. Just wanted to see what you were up to. You haven't seen any kids or teens walking around, have you?"

"No. No one at all," I said. "Just customers for the art studio. Like me."

"Hm. Well, there's been a lotta kids missing from

the reservation over the last year or two." He handed me a photocopied composite of at least a dozen kids' faces along with their information. "I been handin' 'em out. So keep a lookout. Lotta times they just run away, so the law don't help us out much. But still. Thanks."

And with that, he tipped his cap and got into a car that I hadn't even noticed before, which was a bit surprising, considering his car was a gigantic, old, white Cadillac featuring dozens and dozens of objects glued onto the outside of it. Yeah, one of those. Doodads of all kinds were sticking out like porcupine quills in every direction (as he slowly pulled the old caddy forward and drove past, towards town), including dream weavers, Native American tchotchkes, and framed photographs and figurines of everyone from Geronimo to Derek Jeter. *Glued on his car.* Wow. The characters you find down here. In the Southern North.

My peripheral vision detected something was amiss at the art studio, and I turned to look. OK, now those last customers were leaving. That was quick. Their collective expressions read, *"Well, THAT was expensive!"*

"Please," I scoffed at them out loud as I started up my car, "You think you can invest in art while driving a decade-old Prius?" I snickered as I steered my 1992 rusted-out Civic across the street and parked seven unoccupied slots away from the front door of the studio. *Why do I park so far away? I mean, jeez, do I feel unworthy as a fricking human being or what?*

Dutton James was sitting behind the counter of his store, finishing a can of Coke, with his black hair combed nicely when I walked in (I had only seen it wind-blown before, including photos in the paper and on the internets where he always looked as if he had just emerged from gale-force winds). As I entered, he actually opened his eyes this time and looked at me for what I assumed was the first time.

"Hyah! Emma the painter!"

"Wow! You remember me! And you're Dutton James, the sculptor! It's great to see you again!" He looked down and nodded. "Oh, by the way, uh, Littlefeather just told me to say hi? The guy with the crazy car? I just spoke to him." Dutton nodded again.

"You wanna look at my store?"

"Yeah! Definitely!" I looked around. It was like a little, rustic museum shop, except he also had a few small pieces of his actual art for sale, too. There was no sculpture bigger than a bread box, but his work was still fetching big money: $2,500-$15,000 a pop. Wow. Considering the simplicity of the items, his art seemed to be increasing in value before my eyes.

To the side, there were a few piles of tee shirts on shelves with "James Art Studio" printed on them or featuring one of Willow James' paintings, along with her name. $50. *Each.* Wow again. There were mugs behind the counter which Dutton had clearly signed himself that were going for *$200* each! "Oh. Did you sign these?" I asked.

"Yeah, those are with the artist's autograph. I sign

those."

"I see," I said. It was staggering. He could barely write his name, as if he'd autographed them while in a car traveling over a bumpy, dirt road. "And I see," I said, "as per usual, I cannot afford one single thing you're selling."

"Yeah, my art going crazy! I on TV! Eight times! And after I die, it'll be like... Psshw! Pshhw! Pshhw!" (He made a bunch of spitting, flatulent sounds with his mouth which I assumed meant fireworks or something.)

"Yeah, well, unfortunately I can't afford anything you're selling *before* you die either," I assured him.

"You crazy! I got these!" Dutton motioned to a large basket by the cash register. Inside were hundreds, maybe thousands of teeny, cast-off pebbles, similar in look and texture to his larger sculptures. There was a small sign: "$20 each." My God. I couldn't even afford one of his sculpture's shavings!

"Wow. You made all these?" I asked. He guffawed.

"Naw, not really! When I hit it with a chisel, these all over the floor! They like mini art!"

I looked at him with fake surprise. (Actually, maybe not so fake.) "Dutton James. Are you actually selling the trimmings from your art pieces?"

"Hyah! Yeah!"

"Are you selling your garbage for twenty per? Am I gonna find an old shoelace in here?"

"Yeah. It just garbage. It just art!" Dutton exclaimed.

I picked up one of the small clear stones and studied it. What did he use? Some kind of clear, glass-like acrylic? And how did he capture the colors inside them? "Dutton what medium do you use, can I ask?"

"What medum?"

"Medium. It means what ingredients do you use to make these sculptures? Is it...plastic, acrylic?"

"Ha! I never tell!"

I looked up at him, surprised. "What? Why?" I said kiddingly: "What, is it like an illegal substance or something?" His mood shifted, and he looked at the ground. "What is it, some kind of outlawed substance made only in Russia? It's like a see-through rock!"

"Naw. My dad said to not talk to no one about that," Dutton said, quietly.

"Yeah, but..." I pulled out my phone, opened up the Google app, and showed him: "'Dutton James.' See? I can Google your name, and it shows your sculptures —My God... $80,000... Wow... —Anyway, see here? I click on the sculpture, and it shows your medium: *Drip Study 4*. Plastic, glass and acrylic. See?"

"Yeah."

"So how do you mix glass and plastic together? Is it like melted plexiglass? Something like that? Can I see where you make your stuff? Is it in the back somewhere, or...?"

For the first time I ever saw, Dutton rose up totally erect, as he burst up from his chair and ran to a side door. He returned to his slightly hunched posture as he stood in front of it, and bellowed, "No! Dad say no!"

I walked over to one of his sculptures, positioned on a shelf beside him. "I see you make these chisel marks in them." I ran my fingers over the crude, caveman-like gouges in the otherwise pristine, organic (*inorganic?*) form. "I see it doesn't even crack! And those colors inside. Are they acrylic paint? Flash?"

"Yeah."

"Or is it oil paint? Mixed with something like concrete or...mercury or...? What is it? How do you get the reds and the blacks like that?"

"Yeah."

"I'd love to try something like this, Dutton. How do you do it? Can't I have a look?"

"No! *NO!*" shrieked Dutton.

That took me aback. He had a temper. He just showed it. And it wasn't pretty. For the first time, all traces of his naïveté completely vanished. I raised my hands in surrender.

"OK, OK, I guess I'll just take a tee shirt then. Maybe one with your mom's paintings. The one that looks like bleeding flowers."

Dutton walked over to the shirts and raised up a green one featuring his own sculpture printed on it. "This one has my art—"

Immediately, I opened the door to the back room and stepped inside. I had to see. I heard Dutton *roaring and running*, but I slammed the door behind me and put my heel against the bottom. I probably had three or four seconds, tops. I flipped on the light.

I seemed to be in his workroom in the back of

the studio, and it was basically empty. There was one semi-finished sculpture in the corner, and a painting on an easel, showing a flower that looked like it was painted by a three-year-old. That was it, other than a huge metal barrel in the corner, of which some of the contents (some kind of clear liquid) was hardened in drips along the side. Like shellac or something. It had a label on it. Poison.

There was a guttural shout, and then the door partially budged open as Dutton pushed on it, so I lifted my heel and quickly jumped out of the way. The door swung open, and Dutton came tumbling onto the floor, and I nimbly stepped past him.

As I made toward the studio's exit, I passed the basket of chiseled pebbles and pocketed one. *OK, now I've crossed the line between legal and illegal. No more using that excuse anymore.* However, did I just cross another line? The one between kindness and cruelty? After all, I had just essentially pranked a middle-aged autistic man with brain damage. Now he was cursing me out as he picked himself off the floor.

"Dammit, Emma! That not cool! You lie to me! That not cool! You better buy something now or get out!"

"Sorry, I thought I heard something in there..."

"You did not! You lie, Emma! Here, you buy this shirt."

"OK, how much are they? $50?"

"Plus tax!"

"I'm sorry, but I don't have that much on me. Will

you take $17?"

Dutton snatched the shirt off the counter and put it back on the shelf. "Hyah! No way! I lose money for that! My dad take more than half!"

"Your dad?"

"Yeah, he in Boston now. He move back there after my mom die! After both his wifes die! My whole fambily die!"

"Well, you're alive, Dutton."

"He married another lady and she run away and die! So he run away too. He in Boston now, but we talk almost every single day! With FaceTime or Skype!" Dutton suddenly looked down at the basket of sculpture pebbles. "Hey, you take one of these?"

Jesus, I thought. I'd forgotten how some autistic people reportedly have a knack for tabulating presumably uncountable things. Or I was just being paranoid. Either way, it was time to go. "No, of course not!" I said. "OK, you're scaring me a little, Dutton, so I'm going to leave."

"Yeah, get outta here!" Now he was livid, and he was coming towards me.

I grabbed the first thing I could reach to defend myself, which turned out to be Dutton's empty Coke can. I brandished it at him anyway as I opened the front door and squeezed outside. Dutton kept coming. Seeing a group of senior citizens making their way towards the door from a minibus, I relaxed a little.

"Oh look! Some more customers! See you later, Dutton!" I pushed past the seniors, walked quickly to my car, got in, locked the doors, and looked over. Dutton was smiling at his new customers while opening the door for them.

Phew, I thought. *Thank God.* I threw the soda can on the floor of my car (*Who knows when I may need a dangerous weapon again?*) and took the strange, chipped rock out of my pocket to examine it. It was a good specimen. Blue and grey branches inside a see-through stone. What the hell was this stuff? Something from another planet? What the hell was that bizarre-looking barrel in the corner? Some kind of nuclear waste? It didn't look right. I shook my head at the thought and looked up.

My heart stopped as I saw Dutton James staring at me out of the dirty studio window. He was not smiling. I started my car, waved to him, and floored it out of there.

Oh well. There went my fleeting friendship with the one artist who was famous enough to help me out some day.

Way to go, puny Emma.

Adam

Johan Eisengad stood in the lobby of the Math building and glared at me through the large, vented window in the lobby's wall that called itself the Carleton College Office of Administration. I could tell Johan wasn't used to hearing the word, "No."

"*I never signed up for that class!*" he ranted on. "How can I get an F if I wasn't even aware I was in the class? This is going to mess up my GPA! There's no way this can happen!"

"OK, Johan?" I said. "Uh, you did sign up for the class..."

"And I attended the first day! And I didn't like it, so I didn't go back! I dropped the class! Look at the attendance records!"

"OK, Johan? You never officially dropped the class, and we are also talking about last spring!"

"Yeah! I only found out about it this summer when I saw my grades, and there was an F in Sociology!"

"OK, Johan?" I said. "You're going to want to see the dean about this if you want to appeal and have it taken off the record. At this point though, this office can't help you at all." Johan angrily grabbed his papers and stormed away. "Sorry, Johan."

Johan turned back, furiously. "Yeah, RIGHT!!"

Johan spun and strode theatrically across the tiled lobby, flung open the building's front door, and then tried to slam the door with a loud BANG as he exited, but it was one of those unslammable doors that could only inch slowly closed. Johan watched for a bit as the door glacially moved towards closing, then he tried to violently and dramatically force the door closed from the outside (hence, still, "slamming it closed"). But the force was strong with this Math Building's front door, and it didn't vary one iota from its lethargic pace of shutting. Johan glared intensely through the thick, wooden door's small window, and then disappeared, his black cloak whipping the falling orange and yellow leaves behind him, which fluttered like tangerine and lemon vapors until the door finally, quietly clicked shut. Ah youth!

Sometimes working at a school gifts you with wonderful reminders that, often, being young wasn't all that great, and you're left grateful to be thirty-nine-ish. If a preteen is called a "tween," I concluded this made me a "tworty."

Just then, as if the Goddess Aphrodite had arrived to comfort me o'er this debacle, my cell phone rang, showing the name "Emma" over a picture of Ann-Margaret. *My God! She waited practically a month to call me!*

Which meant either Emma was not interested in me, or she was the chillest young woman on earth.

There was only one way to find out. I picked up.

"Hey! Emma! What's up?"

"Adam? Adam Winters? It's Emma Kincaide, remember me?" She sounded frantic and not chill in any way whatsoever. So I guessed she just *wasn't that into me*. Or maybe my whole formula was bull-puckey.

"Sure! Lunch at the art fair and then not a word! What's up?"

"Well, you didn't call me either, so—"

"Wait a minute. I thought your generation of twenty-somethings didn't like the guy calling! I thought I'm supposed to wait for the female to call first. Isn't that a thing now?"

"No, that is definitely not 'a thing'! Who the hell told you that?"

"Uhh... I Asked Jeeves."

"Oh jeez, no wonder," said Emma. "Google it next time."

"I could just ask around for information at the MySpace Lounge or the AOL chat boards..." Silence. I don't think she knew I was kidding. "So! What's up, Emma?"

"Omigod. Listen. I'm in your area. You want to meet at Froggy Bottoms again?"

I checked the time. 11:15. "I could, uh... I could take lunch now..." I said, "but you need to be more specific because you used a shortened nickname. Do you mean Froggy Bottoms River Pub and Lily PADio on Water Street? 'Cuz there are a lot of other establishments with similar names..."

"11:30? See you there. Ciao," said Emma, unamused, and she hung up. I don't think she ever understood even one of my attempts at humor, but she reminded me of a sort of psychotic, bipolar Emma Stone (in a good way), so I'll keep trying.

❖ ❖ ❖

Emma was already seated at a table when I walked in. Her hair looked more crimson and unkempt than I remembered it. "Hey, girl," I said, and she stood up for a quick hug before we sat down. "OK, I'm unclear about something," I said. "Does a millennial pay for the second lunch since I paid for the first, or how does this work?"

Emma glared at me. "Oh, shut up. You're paying for this because I'm broke, not because of my supposed *generation*. Stop assuming there's a bunch of secret generational rules you have to learn! There are no rules! And anybody who is overly rule-based is anally retentive and lame anyway."

"Well, just remember, I Asked Jeeves originally, and he's very rules-based..."

"Yeah, he would be. Listen, I've got something to ask you, and I don't know if you're gonna like it."

"Oh, my sweet, sweet Princess... You had me at 'Oh, shut up' earlier. How may I help you? What, no small talk for Prince Adam?"

Emma rolled her eyes. "Oh, gimme a break. Sorry.

OK: Hey, Adam, it's good to see you again. Sorry I didn't call earlier, but now I just did, alright? Better late than never? There are your prerequisite pleasantries."

"Thank you."

"You're welcome. You want to order?"

I got the attention of the waiter. "Hey, Quentin. Two cheeseburgers and two Cokes? Thanks." Quentin nodded and went to the back. "What's up?" I asked her. "You look weirded out."

"Do you know any people at the Science Department at Carleton? Someone who can do you a favor? It's not a big deal, but I'm a little worried about someone." Emma shut her eyes and smiled, embarrassed, then bowed her head, heaved a heavy sigh, and looked up, opening her eyes again. "Dutton."

"Dutton James?"

"You know someone else named Dutton?"

My eyes narrowed at her sarcasm. "What about Dutton?"

"I just saw him."

"OK...where?"

"At his studio. He got really angry at me."

"What? Why?"

"Oh, I peeked into a back room, and he got all pissy and threw me out."

"Wow!" I exclaimed, amazed and a little impressed.

"It's no big deal," she said, "it's just...Adam, I don't think that dude's an artist."

"What are you talking about?"

"Adam, he can barely even sign his name. I saw a painting he was working on, and it looked as if he had no training or natural talent whatsoever. I'm sorry, but—"

"Maybe it wasn't his painting."

She glared at me. "Who else works there?"

"Uh... nobody. His sister Lily's not an artist at all, and she lives in Wisconsin, and his dad lives in Boston. Actually, I do remember Dutton's dad was an artist once, but when his wife became The Famous Willow James, I think he stopped. Couldn't take it."

"He was envious of her. Also known as *'freudenschade,'*" said Emma.

"*Gesundheit.* Yeah, I'm beginning to remember our other lunch now. I think that was your new word of the day."

"Oh, shut up."

"Again with the shutting up..."

"Stop being defensive, Adam. Listen, I don't think Dutton knows the first thing about art! He's going to get ground to dust by the press!"

"Well, that's what a savant is! Right? He just knows! He's a *wunderkind*!"

"He's not a kid..." she mumbled.

"The art speaks for him!" I went on. "It's not like he's doing realistic, Rodin-type sculptures! They're totally abstract! It's like he creates...*reflections of his own mind.* That's what I always thought, anyway."

"Well, be that as it may, he isn't living like a person

with a lot of means or money. He said his dad takes half of everything, so I wonder if he's ripping him off or something. What's Dutton's house like?"

"You saw it."

"What? He *lives at the studio?*"

I shrugged.

"Wow," said Emma. "There must have been more rooms back there because his working studio was practically empty! And something concerned me too. There was a barrel of what seemed to be some pretty toxic stuff. I think I saw a skull on the side, y'know, like signifying poison."

"Well, turpentine is poison... paint thinner... even papier mâché if you drank gallons of it..."

"Shut up," Emma said again, taking a small rock out of her pocket and laying it on the table. "That's a piece of Dutton's sculptures. He probably sells them to make ends meet because his dad hasn't conceived of the idea yet that Dutton could charge money for his fricking garbage. I want you to find out what this is made of."

I blinked. "I beg your pardon? Me?"

"Yeah! With your Carleton...science...connections...!"

"Uhhh. I don't know if they can do that..."

"Sure they can! That's beginner stuff! Easy! C'mon!" Emma grabbed her phone and started poking all over it.

"Look, I'll ask," I said, "but it might take a while, if they can do it at all."

"Sure, I understand..." she said, still searching through her phone, "I was looking at Willow's old works while I was waiting for you. Have you seen them?"

"Sure, I've seen a bit. She gifted one painting to the Carleton Gallery before she died that's pretty cool, sort of scary or satanic or—"

"Look at this!" Emma laid her phone on the table and swiped through multiple images of the late Willow James herself; dark, imposing-looking, with black hair in her early years and grey hair with black streaks in her latter ones. Emma swiped on to her paintings. They were twisted and macabre but with bold, bright colors; darker-than-blacks, and juicy reds, featuring all sorts of physical objects attached, like newspaper clippings, or treated, rotted wood, or jagged, metallic chunks. Oftentimes, it looked as if she was trying to destroy her own work during its creation, yet, still, it absolutely stood out as great, thrilling art. Authentic beauty. The kind that put your mind in a state of reverential awe. "See this here?" added Emma as if reading my mind, "These pieces where she's actually dissolving the canvas and paint? That must be something like sulfuric acid. Maybe there was some left over there from after she died. Dutton couldn't handle something like that. You can't even breathe around it! And frankly, he doesn't look well. He's got, like, dark rings under his eyes now. And both times I've seen him, he references his own death like it's something funny! I mean, what happened to his mom? How did Willow James die?"

"She drowned herself."

"Right. She pulled a Virginia Woolf, and weighted herself down with stones, and walked into one of Minnesota's 10,000 lakes. That's what Wikipedia says too. That's what her bio says too. But if you read other stuff..."

"What, like conspiracy stuff?"

"Adam, she may have been killed. They never found her body. It was her husband's word along with his new wife's. What if they wanted to cash in on her art and killed her? Like Dutton keeps saying, the value of art skyrockets when the artist dies."

"Dutton actually said 'skyrocket'?" I asked.

"No, but he made, like, fireworks noises or something. Adam...I wonder if Willow James left some of her own sculptures behind for Dutton with instructions on how and when to release them. I think Willow created Dutton's sculptures over twenty years ago."

"And then she hid them?" I asked her. Emma sat back and nodded. "And where on your fancy phone is any of Willow James' artwork that looks anything like Dutton's?"

She shook her head. "There isn't any."

I leaned back in my chair and studied her while Quentin brought us our burgers and left.

"So what do you think?" Emma asked, "Am I crazy? Supposedly, you look out for Dutton, don't you? Aren't you the least bit worried about him?"

She got me there. I picked up the strange, small

rock. "OK, you've nearly convinced me. I'll ask a Carleton science guy I know if a chemical test is in any way doable. But that means you owe me, Miss No-Call."

"I owe *you*? That's OK, I've already got that figured out: I noticed that the Northfield theater is showing at least two movies I want to see. I haven't seen a film since I was living in Chicago. So after you buy these burgers, you're then going to pay for us to see a movie. You can call in sick at work. And I don't like popcorn, but you can buy me Junior Mints. OK? There. I owed you, and now we're even."

We looked at each other for a long time, chewing over our burgers and her nonsensical math equation. I took a sip of Coke.

"OK," I said. "Thanks."

"You're welcome."

Sheriff Janssen

The sheriff hoisted his arms above his head and clicked off a photo of the inside of the restaurant, lowered his sunglasses to check that he'd captured her, and then pressed a few buttons. His phone made a "swishing" sound, and he spoke into it.

"OK, I just took a picture with my Samsung, and I sent it to ya."

The voice on the other end said, "I ain't got nothin'." There was a *ding*-ing sound. "OK, now I got it."

Sheriff Janssen's finger poked his sunglasses back over his eyes, and he checked-out Northfield's main drag, Division Street. Everything looked A-OK. He spoke into the Samsung: "Is that her?"

"Yeah, that's her," came the voice on the other end.

"Well, I'll keep an eye on her, but I don't think she amounts to nothin'."

"Oh yeah?"

"Yeah. I think the James boy told me she was an artist or whatnot," said the sheriff, "And that's sure what she looks like to me. Like a whole lotta nothin'."

"Not from the government?"

"Nah, I don't think so... The Winters boy is seein'

her though, no doubt about that."

"Oh, yeah? The quarterback?"

"Yeah. I ain't seen her here but twice, and both times he's had his butter-fingered talons inside her. I think that's the extent of her interest in this town."

In Ripo Lake, Samuel Lightfeather took the sheriff off speakerphone. "OK, then. She sure seemed interested in somethin' out here though, whether it be the reservation or the James boy."

"Well, he ain't no boy," muttered the sheriff. "Dutton must be in his late thirties by now…"

"*You* just called him the James boy!"

"Well, I dunno," said the sheriff. "He sure acts like it."

"Don't I know it."

"I'll keep an eye on her and report back if there's anything else, alright, Sam?"

"Yeah, OK," answered Samuel Flying Lightfeather and hung up.

Sheriff Julius Janssen dropped his phone into his pocket, hitched up his baggy, brown uniform pants ("They don't chafe my undercarriage if they're baggy," he was known to say from time to time), and started waddle-walking down the sidewalk, shuffling yellow leaves in front of him along the way, and surveying his kingdom, population 2,020. He frowned when a thought occurred. "Say there, Janice, I don't suppose the Willow James family is related to Jesse James, are they?"

Mrs. Mayhew shook her head. "Naw. They moved

here from Massachusetts or Connecticut or somesuch place."

"Oh, that's right," recalled the sheriff. They walked further in silence. "Say, Janice, keep an eye on the Froggy Bottoms River Pub and Lily PADio, wouldya, and tell me when the Winters boy and that redheaded stepchild step out, willya?"

"Yeah, OK," replied Mrs. Mayhew, pivoting her roundish body around to check the street. Nobody exiting Froggy Bottoms River Pub and Lily PADio at that point.

"Why doncha just park it on this bench for a spell and contact me on the two-way when they leave? Ya don't have to keep dogging my every step, woman." The sheriff's strong Minnesota accent tended to become thicker when simmered with a dash of anger, Mrs. Mayhew could attest to that.

"OK," she answered, dropping her burly behind on the bench outside the Northfield Bank while the sheriff walked on.

Frankly, Janice Mayhew was relieved. It seemed they were both growing ashamed to be seen beside one another in public. *Oh, look, there's Sheriff Janssen and Deputy Mayhew, he in his full sheriff uniform and she always in plain clothes and holding a clipboard.* He always swore he was ordering a uniform for her, but she started there a full year and a half ago now! She figured it was because they both knew how ridiculous she'd look in a police outfit.

Even though Janice Mayhew had passed all the police academy tests, which is something she decided to do as a late-in-life, ex-gym-teacher's second act following her husband's elopement with his *travel agent* (who the criminey has a travel agent anymore!?), her present occupation was more as the "sheriff's assistant," really. As Sheriff Julius asked her once, "You ever see a uniformed police officer hangin' out with a plain-clothes one on the boob tube? Only when one of 'em is a *detective*, and you ain't no *detective*! It's perception that matters, and if nobody ain't ever seen it before, they ain't gonna know what to make of it!' (His thick Minnesota tongue had been practically indecipherable during that particular outburst.) So as a result of these forked words, Mrs. Mayhew was perpetually trying to stay off in the shadows, yet always somehow be nearby if needed. She was like a spy. *Maybe more like a Secret Shopper,* she figured. It was a fine line, really.

Sheriff Janssen approached The Northfield Bank Museum and looked in the window. It was empty, it being a school day, and during working hours and all. Normally, the sheriff would have bristled at a museum commemorating a villainous scofflaw like Jesse James, but it really stood as more of a memorial to his own police force.

Because Northfield, Minnesota was the place that famously put a stop to Jesse James. Even made a movie about it: *The Great Northfield, Minnesota Raid*, starring none other than Robert Duvall. That was in 1971 (Sheriff Janssen actually met Mr. Duvall and Mr. Cliff Robertson, who played the outlaw, Cole

Younger. In the sheriff's opinion, Mr. Duvall was always a little too much in character, a scary thought considering he was embodying the murderous Jesse James, and Cliff Robertson, though probably the handsomest man the sheriff ever saw, just seemed drunk all the time. Still, it was a proud time for Northfield). One of the sheriff's most gratifying moments.

In fact, Sheriff Julius always thought Northfield's town sign should have echoed its proud anti-Jesse James legacy by adding another C-word to it. To wit: "Home of Cows, Colleges, Contentment...and Catching Jesse James." He wasn't sure where in the order it should appear—maybe it could even move up the list—but for Chrissakes, who the hell chose to put "*Cows*" first, anyway? *Oh that's right*, the sheriff recalled, *it was that artsy librarian from Duluth who came up with the sign's slogan.* And then, much to his chagrin, it was voted in. That was NOT a banner day for Northfield because it made the small town fodder for mockery from the big cities. Oh well, the sheriff couldn't do *everything* himself, could he? Seemed he spent his whole life promoting and protecting Northfield, nurturing it like his own flesh and blood for so, so many, many decades now. Yes, this town certainly would be his lasting legacy. And he figured that wasn't too shabby.

His radio belched and Mrs. Mayhew's voice crackled out: "Sheriff, they're stepping out now."

Janssen reversed his direction at a brisker pace. "Alright, Janice."

As the Winters boy and his fiery-haired vixen neared, the sheriff feigned surprise. "Oh! Hello, Mr. Winters."

"Hey, Sheriff," said Adam. "What's shakin'?"

"Oh well, I don't know about that... Now ain'tcha gonna introduce me to your friend?"

"Uh... this is Emma, and... I forgot your last name," Adam admitted to Emma, embarrassed.

"Kincaide. Nice to meet you. I live up in Fargo."

"Oh yeah? What are ya doin' down here?" asked the sheriff.

"Just... interested in the arts, I guess."

Mrs. Mayhew chimed in: "Ain't gonna be another art fair 'til next spring."

"Dammit, Janice, why are here and speakin'?"

"Well, you told me to sit on this bench, and then you all just stopped right here, gabbing away. Never mind." Mrs. Mayhew looked down at her crotch area.

The sheriff attempted a smiley-ish thing on his lower face. "Where ya goin'?" he asked. "Maybe I can walk with ya a ways."

"Just to the shuttle for the movie theatre," said Adam.

"Oh, yeah?" piped Mrs. Mayhew. "Whatcha gonna see?"

"Janice!" the sheriff barked. Mrs. Mayhew returned to her groin while the sheriff led Adam and Emma down the sidewalk toward the shuttle stop. "Just wanted to know if maybe you was with the government in some way or somethin', seein' as you was hangin' out by the reservation today..."

"Holy crap! Who told you that?" asked Emma, "Dutton?"

"Oh, did you see Dutton James today?"

"Yeah. So?" asked Emma, a little shaken.

"Nothin' to it, Miss Thing, nothin' to it; just wanted to know who's passing through is all. No great shakes."

Adam looked darkly at the sheriff and said, "Watch out, Emma. There's a lot of gossip and poison in this town."

The sheriff tipped his hat and walked away. "You have a good day, Mr. Winters." As he passed the bank, Mrs. Mayhew mumbled: "Did you just call her 'Miss Thing'?"

"Shut up, Janice."

Dan Auerbach

Dan's face crinkled into an orange, snakeskin-leathered smile. "That's right. Next month. The week of December tenth through the seventeenth to be exact. At the Perriman Gallery in New York City."

"And what's his name again, for people who just tuned in?"

"He's Willow James' only son, his name is Dutton James, and he's a real talent to be reckoned with."

"And he's your son too, isn't that right?"

Dan smiled again. "And I couldn't be prouder, Jack."

"As long as we're on the subject of Willow James, you were married to her for, what, eighteen, nineteen years?"

Dan's buoyant demeanor altered a bit, but he maintained eye contact with Wild Morning Jack of WMMI, Boston. This was not one of the agreed-upon subjects. But it was live radio so what was he going to do?

"Yes, Jack, that's right."

"I just have to ask, *what was she like?* Willow James? The demon lady? Or so nicknamed from her most famous painting, *Demon Lady*, which everybody assumes was based on herself?"

"Y'know, it's funny. She never admitted to any of her paintings being autobiographical in nature—"

"Well, we know she never spoke much about her work, but my question is, *what was it like? Living with the actual Demon Lady?* I mean, let's face it, she was pretty hot." Wild Jack pressed a button on the console; A cartoonish wolf-whistle sounded. "With all due respect, I mean, we can talk, can't we? Just be guys? I mean, take me through a day in the Willow James/Dan Auerbach household of old. You woke up, what happened?"

Dan wondered if this was sweeps week, or radio's equivalent of it, because this guy was clearly going for gold. "Well, let's see," said Dan. "Willow would always be up very early, and in her studio. She didn't like to be disturbed. I was always more the business end of things. Even after she died, I've represented her estate and the lion's share of her work. But we had some great times in the early days. Great times. She was a sweetheart. As time wore on, however, I think she became more of a...tortured soul, I guess?"

There. Was that enough red meat for your listeners, Wild Jack? Dan guessed not, since Jack was readying a follow up. Evidently, the groundlings weren't satisfied yet, and the great unwashed needed more dirt.

"How much are you worth, man?" asked Jack.

Instantly, Jack's sidekick, Lil' Marco, threw up his arms and bellowed: "Oooooh!!!"

Dan's face turned a rich, deep-red color inclining to purple. "Oh, you know. I do alright."

Wild Jack persisted: "It's not like it's a secret! How many times have you been on that *Forbes* list for Richest People? Ten times?"

Dan smiled. He secretly enjoyed this particular line of questioning because, let's face it, *Wasn't this what it was all about?* "I don't know," said Dan. "A few!" (Laughing with Wild Jack and Marco.) "I've been on the list a few times!" (Gracefully waiting for the laughter to subdue.) "But we're at another level now, Jack. This kid, Dutton James. Well, you've seen his work..."

"It is amazing. It is," said a tamer Jack now, dropping character for the first time in the interview and speaking as he were legitimately carbon-based. "It's just off the hook. I mean it's space age, it's otherworldly, and the fact he's reportedly now installing lighting *inside* the sculptures...? The peek I've had at his new stuff...he is really takin' it to the next level. Like, y'know when you're in the *aquarium? And you go to that dark, neon-looking, 3-D jellyfish room?*"

"Gotta go there when you're high!" chipped in Lil' Marco.

"True that. But the insane, uh, psychedelic colors, that's the only thing I can compare it to. Jellyfish. And when have you people *ever heard me talk about ART!?*" (Lil' Marco cackled and bellowed again.) "I mean, that's how good this stuff is. And his name is Dutton James. And he'll be in New York City starting

December tenth, followed, reportedly, by an auction at Sotheby's, but don't show up there unless you the type who's got a million dollars in your couch cushions, you know what I mean?" Marco bellowed and Jack howled. "You gotta be in the upper, UPPER tenth of one percent to afford this stuff, you feel me?"

Well, Dan thought, *maybe this interview wasn't such a bad idea after all.* "Perhaps someday, Jack," Dan added, "we'll be talking in the multi-millions of dollars per piece. SO, for anybody who attends, it's a chance at a great, great investment opportunity. I mean, look at what's happened here. Dutton has autism. Yet he was anointed by the gods of art with immense talent. Dutton's a special guy. And frankly, we want him to hang around for as long as he can. We just want to enjoy him *while he's here*, and that's really the bottom line of what we're talking about." Dan leaned back in his chair, feeling all warm and gooey. *Perfection,* he thought.

Wild Jack howled. "I wanna thank The Silver Jackal for coming here and tellin' us what's up in the cultured world because we Wild Jack Animals need some culture!" Jack pressed a button. Fart noise. Marco bellowed again. "Alright, we back, we back. But we also gotta pay some bills. Y'all keep it here on 97.8 WMMI, The Morning Jack. It's 8:51."

Wild Jack stood up and shook Dan's hand while a loud ad for a Boston law firm blared over the speakers. Dan laid his headphones down and quickly walked out while checking his phone. Two missed calls from Lily, his daughter in Wisconsin. He speed-dialed her back while rushing out the door, not wishing to be delayed over sundry, trifling matters like his signature on a release for the interview (which just aired live anyway) demanded by some ludicrous radio station lawyer. Lily answered quickly.

"Daddy?"

"Hey, honey. Were you listening?"

"Yeah, Dad? Are you sure Dutton's ready for this? I mean, the last time I talked to him...he's not getting any better, and maybe getting worse. Is he on his meds?"

"He says he doesn't like them," said Dan.

Lily sighed. "Dad, you gotta get him back on his meds if he's going to be meeting rich people in New York City! He'll be a huge joke!"

"He's not coming to New York."

"Oh, and since when was this decided? Because you know Dutton thinks he's going!"

"No, no. Dutton was never going to go," insisted Dan while stepping around a kissing couple outside a Shake Shack. "Better he stay in Minnesota and run his little shop. I took everything of any value away a long time ago anyway. And now, we're installing halogen lights in the sculptures and placing them all on $10,000 mounts. It's all just stunning. It really is."

"How much are you going to ask for them?"

"We should clear millions by the time it's all over, Lily. At least I hope so. We've got over fifty pieces, for God's sake."

"Alright, well, I'm relieved he's not going to New

York. Dutton's my little brother, Dad, and I couldn't see how—"

"Just don't tell him."

"What?" Lily seemed surprised.

Dan ducked off the sidewalk into a Barney's entrance, away from the flow of pedestrians, and spoke in a calm hush. "We're not going to tell Dutton at all. We're going to tell him his exhibit was delayed until next year, and that everything's going smoothly. We'll need someone to be with Dutton too, that week, to make sure he doesn't see any newspapers or talk to anyone. I contacted Sheriff Janssen, but he can't do much. It's not like he can arrest him and lock him in a cell or anything. Although, frankly, I don't see why not... Maybe you could visit him up there that week?"

Lily made a noise like she was being choked. "I—I—I—No, Dad, I've got the boys, I can't just—"

"Bring 'em. Make it a vacation. On my dime. Take Dutton to the Twin Cities. See some comedy shows. Just distract him. I'll get my secretary to send you plane tickets. Deal?"

Lily hesitated slightly until, like always with her dad, she melted into this pathetic puddle of dirty-blonde, tepid, daughter juice.

"OK, Daddy. I will."

"Thanks, angel."

Maya

Maya smiled and grimaced equally as she received her massage, her mind going a hundred miles a minute, at least.

So now Dan Auerbach was taking eighty percent. A new record for gouging.

But...

Say the whole lot sold for thirty million at Sotheby's? What's twenty percent of that?

The answer is six million dollars. All going to Maya. She could retire at fifty-two. This was exactly what she needed. This was Endgame Money.

And Kira? Well, she could trade her in for a newer model. Sounded callous, but there it was.

Maya gazed over Manhattan and at the bright, brilliant red leaves floating off the trees in Central Park, whisked into wide circles while they struggled to stay up in the air to remain relevant. Normally, a gallery would take fifty percent of what they sold, forty percent if it really seemed an artist had true talent. But the Silver Jackal was the only one who ever made the absurd leap to allotting only thirty percent to the gallery to sell Willow's paintings. Dan's late second wife Linda wanted to give only a twenty percent cut to the gallery, but luckily that never happened back then (because Maya had her murdered, although no one but Kira knew about *that*), and Maya and Dan finally agreed to a seventy-thirty split.

This was now, though, and even though Dan was presently adamant he would only fork over a measly twenty percent commission for the gallery to sell Dutton's sculptures, it didn't seem so outrageous to Maya anymore. Maya was finished with this life, *and there was going to be plenty of money to go around*, she figured. Hey, all she needed was that six million. *Too bad for the kid though*, she thought, because she doubted Dutton would see much of any money at all.

Ever since Dutton signed the trust that gave Dan Auerbach custody and complete control of the entire James estate, it meant *only Dan Auerbach, alone, controlled ALL the money.* And just the same way Dan wasn't willing to fork over a fortune to Willow when she was exhibiting signs of early-onset mania, he wasn't now going to entrust a king's ransom to his son with autism and possible brain damage from his run-in with a garbage truck either.

Maya smirked at Dan's sweet deal. Dan Auerbach was also the agent of his artists, which meant he was *supposed* to scoop off yet another twenty percent of their take for himself, but it was rumored that Dan routinely took over fifty percent! Truly unheard of.

And who were the only clients he's ever had? Maya thought, *Willow and Dutton James. Two artists whose work was so unapologetically daring and brashly un-*

usual, you either hated it at first glance, or loved it so much you felt your life was forever altered, whether for better or worse. Maya's own unofficial market research on the reaction to Willow James' art on typical viewers was seventy-five percent enthralled, to twenty-five percent appalled. Those were excellent stats for any risk-taking artist. On the other hand, Dutton's overall positive reaction from viewers across the board seemed more like an astounding ninety-ten split. Maya had never seen anything like that. *If there ever existed anything that could be deemed a "sure thing" in this ridiculously subjective, back-biting, front-stabbing, and high-paying art world, this was it.*

"That's it," groaned Maya against the pain. "Right there. Harder." The masseuse redoubled her Amazon-like efforts on Maya's lower back.

Maya was admittedly surprised when Dan signed the contract she presented him, unamended. Because there was a well-disguised clause, buried deep within that could net Maya a much greater payout. She was positively floored when Dan didn't object to it. Maybe he didn't have all those lawyers looking after his interests like he always claimed he did.

No matter what happened though, outside of some unforeseen, catastrophic event, Maya was sure to cash in big. She could probably buy an island somewhere and be living there by June. And then she would be single and liberated and happy for the first time in decades. Maya could finally shake free of all her dirty little secrets, and the loathsome things she had to do to get ahead (at a much younger age, Maya once actually had to give Dan Auerbach a blowjob. *And then she simply continued doing business with him for thirty years! I mean Jesus!*). Her mind would at last be purged of all the borderline-illegal decisions and resulting borderline-illegal actions she made over the years (some not-so borderline), and finally, she would be forever free from all the pettiness she had to suffer and discover within herself from three decades in this soul-devouring, heart-decimating, holocaust masquerading as a business, ironically referred to as the Fine Arts.

Maya smiled. She liked her new number-one goal: She needed to be settled in with some twenty-year-old titty-queen on her own, hurricane-free, private island by June.

"Good enough," groaned Maya, slowly turning on to her back. "Now give me the Robert Kraft Happy Ending, and bone me like a herring."

CHAPTER 3
(December)

Dutton

I like Lily. She a good sister. "Hyah! I like this funny guy!"

Lily talk. "Yeah? I liked the first guy better, but he's pretty good too." She smile. "I'm really happy to be here with you, Dutton. I love you so much. You know that, don't you?" She look at me with water in her eyes. She crying?

"Are you crying?" She laugh and touch the ends of her black drippy eyes with one finger so the other fingers stretch out like peacocks.

"I'm sorry...I'm just...Dutton, do you know how proud I am of you? You're my little brother. I love you so much."

"Excuse me, am I interrupting your conversation over here?" The funny guy on the stage look at Lily like he was mad now. "Listen, I don't go to his job and razz him while he flips burgers, and I don't come to your place of work and knock the dick out of your mouth, so how 'bout shutting up?" Lily stand up mad.

"Nice fricking mouth, asshole, and real original goddamn joke! Is that the only ad lib you comedians have?"

"Oh, well I see this has been a problem with you before!" People laugh.

"Come on, Dutton, let's go." She bend and hold my arm but I don't like being touched.

"No, I want to stay!"

"Come on, get your coat."

"Yeah, get your coat, Rain Man. *People's Court* is on in fifteen minutes." (They laugh and I feel prickles and my face burns and I scream at jerky man.)

"YOU SHUT UP!! This my SISTER!! You don't TALK LIKE THAT!! This LILY!! You a BAD MAN!!" I want to kill his face and now I am going at him and people hold my body and I don't like being touched. Big guys in black shirts take us outside but I still screaming.

We on the side now, sidewalking now. Lily smile sad.

"Sorry, Dutton, that was my fault. I shouldn't have been talking so loud. I just want you to know I love you." I shut my eyes.

"I know! Duh. We don't go there again!"

"That's right! We'll never go to Dudley Riggs again!" We still walking.

"You hungry?" My blonde hair sister pretty when she talk and smile 'cuz she don't look tired and old then. I nod head 'cuz I hungry. "Want to get something to eat? Maybe see a movie and then head back to the hotel and see your nephews?" I so happy I hug her but only for one second. "OK, sweetie, we'll do that. And then tomorrow we'll go to museums with the kids. We'll go see Mom's paintings at the Walker!" She put her hand and hold my hand and I let her. "Just don't ever forget, no matter what ever happens to us, that I love you, and I am so unbelievably proud of you!"

"For what?"

"Well, for your artwork! Do you know how *famous* you are now, Dutton? There are articles about you all over the place! You were on the cover of *Art Forum*! You're getting huge! I know Dad doesn't allow you to do interviews, but still! Must be exciting!"

"I never have money with art. It just art."

"Well...we'll make sure Dad gives you more money from now on. You hear me? He gives me and the kids money all the time! Especially when he sells a bunch of our family's art, *which is what he's about to do!* You have earned yourself a lot of money, Dutton, and I'm going to see you get it."

"Yeah."

"You hear me?"

"Yeah."

I know my sister love me.

She the only one in the world.

Emma

"I'm good, aren't I? Of course I am!"

I've always felt it was better to talk out loud to myself. It was somehow both soothing and more likely to inspire action. I looked at my paintings stacked on the passenger seat of my Civic. Oil paintings of sunrises and farmhouses and lakes and interesting faces.

Then I thought of the artwork created by one Dutton James, and I got so angry and full of *freudenschieist* or whatever, that I had to pull the car over so I could *breathe*. Then I just sat there with my head down. For ten minutes or more. *Why was this so personal to me?* There were a few obvious reasons:

Number one, this was my lifelong career choice that we were talking about here. The creation of art! It decided whether I was worthy at what I chose to DO for the rest of my life! *Of course it's going to bother me if my work, when compared with the best, doesn't even stand up! It's depressing, and it's scary! Because if I don't have what it takes, then how the hell does that reflect on the rest of my LIFE?! Can I even survive?*

Number two. I meticulously and exhaustively studied the artwork of both Willow and Dutton

James over the past few months. I tried desperately to draw inspiration from it and inject more life and genius into my artwork. I saw that I needed to take more risks, suffer more pain, create greater beauty, and be less anal about what was or wasn't stylistically "normal" (and depend less on the basics of my training) in order to encourage rampant experimentalism. I needed to have more fun when producing art, ingest more and/or different drugs, ingest less/zero drugs, listen to Mozart while I paint, listen to ear-splitting thrash punk while I paint, paint indoors, outdoors, alone, in public, paint while angry, paint while happy, and paint emotionlessly. I still couldn't find the "*it*". Simply put, my work did not rise head and shoulders above the rest and shout out, *I'm different! I'm awesome!* Maybe with practice it would come. But what would I do in the meantime? Starve? Plus, most artists accomplish their greatest works when they're young, or they may not ever! Mozart was brilliant when he was a child! Which leads me to the most perplexing reason for my discontent...

Number three. How can an untrained, mentally challenged man-boy create mind-bogglingly, awe-inspiring things, and I CAN'T!? Yeah, right, I know, the whole Amadeus-Salieri-savant-*wunderkind*-thing. That. *Fine.* OK. *So? What's up with that? What is it?* God's little joke? I thought "good things come to those who work"? (Or is it "to those who wait"? Well, I didn't have time to "wait" anyway because I'm living in my childhood room at Grandma's house for cripe's sake!)

Drifting back to reality, I raised my head. Where was I now? I checked my phone's GPS. Only a few miles from the border of the reservation. "And this time," I spoke aloud, "I will park my car legally, on public land. So there. And only THEN will I systematically commit seven dozen illegal acts. So. *The greatest. Plan. Ever.*"

I parked off the main road, on the far side of a dark, unlit, dirt path leading God knows where, got out of my car, and silently closed the door and locked it. Now I was outside, starkly alone. No large metal box to shield me.

I picked my way through the woods when I could, and noiselessly dashed across small fields when I couldn't, trying to follow along the road toward the town of Ripo Lake (all the while dodging every streetlight I saw). It was around three a.m. now, and only a handful of cars passed by, all seemingly creeping along as quietly and shamefully as I (*What were they doing driving around at three a.m. anyway!?*).

I'd previously deduced it would be no more than half an hour on foot, but it ended up being over an hour, and it felt like twelve. I was cold, yet sweating profusely, which seemed to make me feel even more chilled. I thought about turning back many times, but always kept going, figuring that if it took *x many minutes* to get here, it would then take that long to get back anyway, so why go back empty-handed if I'm already this far?

Finally, I recognized the section of the road where

I sat in my car months before, across from The James Art Studio. As I approached the dark building, I was surprised to see fences in the process of being built around the outskirts of the property. In the moonlight, it looked like a shadowy, onerous obstacle course to be conquered in near darkness. Superb.

I remained hidden behind bushes for a good few minutes, trying to sense if there was anybody lurking about, and straining to see where the cameras were that caused Mr. Lightfeather to question me before. Evidently, they took trespassing very seriously around here, seeing as they alerted that Joe Arpaio-policeman about it *mere minutes later*. I tried to visualize the most efficient, least intrusive path to the back of the studio. One more moment of listening...

Nothing.

I took a deep breath, softly and shakily let it out, and moved.

I silently traversed a wide circle around to the very back of the property, then made my way through the shadows to the back wall of the studio, stepping slowly and gingerly around any obstacle. I was hoping Dutton's living quarters would be located in the rear, judging from the peek I got at his backroom art studio.

There were only two windows in the back of the studio, so I peeked into the closest one and saw nothing but pitch blackness. Hoping to God the moonlight better illuminated the other window, I quietly picked my way over to it, peered in, and saw what looked to be an unmade, empty bed. Good. So hopefully Adam was right: Dutton was gone for the weekend with his sister.

I tried to open the window. Locked. Carefully removing my cell phone from my pocket (and remembering to cover it with my hand), I switched on the flashlight feature. Even smothered by my hand, the dim light was like the blaze from 1,000 suns illuminating my shameful, stupid actions for all of mankind to see. Quickly, I pointed it into the window.

Inside I saw a sad, filthy, makeshift bedroom. The floor was partially torn out, with jagged shards of sheet metal sticking up in every direction, casting eerie, almost daunting shadows along the far wall. It was only then that I realized for the first time that this was not a regular building with a concrete foundation and plaster walls, it was more like a large metal warehouse, partitioned into several sections with painted drywall. The flooring in this back area was little more than a slightly raised steel sheet on stilts covered by moldy, filthy rugs. Where the floor was broken open, a few throw rugs rested atop the bending, sharp metal fingers, presumably to protect Dutton from being shredded to ribbons if his arm happened to graze them.

I pressed my face against the window and raised the light beam above my head, straining to see the other side of the room, but I didn't have the angle. Stifling the phone's light by firmly compressing it under my armpit, I crept back to the first window again. Cautiously, I laid the light upon the window.

Then I gasped out loud at what I saw.

Dutton had been digging. There were shovels of different sizes stuck into the dirt underneath the ripped-open, metal floor.

And in one area, in the middle of the floor, I could see what he was doing. He was burying them! He was burying his sculptures! And there were more, smaller sculptures partially concealed in the walls!

My mind tried to make sense of it. Why would he do that? Maybe out of paranoia? He was, after all, in the process of having the property lined with tall fences. Maybe people had been snooping around (like me, I guiltily admitted to myself). Was he stockpiling his work, like his father was said to have done when he released dozens of Willow's paintings, years after her death? That didn't seem like anything Dutton could conceive of, let alone do. *Maybe his father told him to?*

Whatever the answer to this burning question was, it would have to wait because my heart ceased functioning when I suddenly saw the entire wall lit up in a red, white, and blue glow. A loud WHOOP sounded, jump-starting my heart back into motion and over-accelerating its beating until I could feel it in my ears, causing the whole of my body to involuntarily shake so hard I couldn't even stand still.

I turned around and saw two police cars shining blinding, blinking, flashing, turning lights and silhouetting that old policeman from Northfield and two other cops wearing different kinds of uniforms, who were pointing guns at me and shouting something. Standing to the side was the Native American man I met before, Mr. Lightfeather.

My startled, jumbled brain tried to understand what they were shouting at me. They were saying to get on the ground. They were pointing guns at me. They looked nervous.

I got on the ground. They were saying to put my hands behind my head. So I did, but they were *still pointing guns at me and kept doing it*, and they still looked nervous.

I heard and felt their footsteps rapidly approach, and then someone grabbed my hands very roughly and secured them together behind my back in some kind of tight restraint. The last voice I heard was the gravelly tone of the old Northfield policeman.

"Well, looky who showed up here again? The red-headed stepchild."

Adam

I couldn't imagine who was calling me at four-fifteen a.m., but even in my sleep state, I knew it was something either very bad, or very important. When I walked into the Ripo Lake Police Department's offices half an hour later, I was unpleasantly greeted by the sight of Sheriff Julius Janssen leaning against a wall.

"Hello, Sheriff," I said. "What are you doing here? This is miles from your jurisdiction, isn't it?"

"Oh, this matter concerns *me*, Mr. Winters, in every sense of the word. *It concerns me greatly*." The corners of his mouth curled up, and for the first time I could remember, I saw his whole face when he smiled, without his sunglasses on. The skin around his eyes looked weathered and haggard, ravaged by a lifetime of self-inflicted stress and worry. His eyes spoke of stubborn over-confidence, and perhaps a little meanness as he attempted a smirk. I decided I liked and trusted him even less than I thought. He went on: "And you, the perpetrator's boyfriend, being a lifelong *bona fide* Northfield native with all the bells and trimmings and all, I thought we could have a word or two. You don't mind, do you?"

"I don't see how I could help since—"

"Well, that might just be the truest thing you ever said, Adam. My good friend, Adam Winters. Quarterback extraordinaire."

Wow. He was going right for the jugular tonight.

I said, "OK, from what I understand, you're going to release her into my custody now or...?"

"Seems to be the case. Now, we will eventually charge her for trespassing on private property, but seems we can't slap her with a felony, since she wasn't actually breaking and entering... *Yet.*" Sheriff Janssen shot a quick, dirty look at the youngest officer present, who cowered like an abused mutt. The sheriff continued, "See, I get the strong feeling she would have tried to break in if we waited a little longer, seeing as she had a YouTube video stored on her Apple and all, showing various ways to pick a door's lock, but this wasn't my show, so as a result, we merely caught Miss Emily Astrid Kincaide peeking into the windows at the James Art Studio. That there's only a misdemeanor so we can't hold her. She claims she was retrieving one of her own paintings she left with Dutton at his studio, but that doesn't really explain why she was wearing a backpack with two of her paintings inside. I have my suspicions, but nothing I can prove... *Yet.*" This time Sheriff Janssen didn't glare at the young officer, but the newbie patrolman shrank down a bit all the same, as if Pavlov's dog heard a bell signaling a beating. "Since she's twenty-one years old," added the sheriff, "we don't need to call her parents, although I've been leanin' toward that being a good thing. But she said to call *you*, and I guess there's standard laws and cookie-cutter statutes and suchforth that allow her the rights to do such things."

"Does Dutton know yet?" I asked.

Sheriff Janssen made a sour face. "I don't think I'm gonna say anything at all to Dutton about this 'cuz God only knows how he'd overreact, with his mind and all. So you gonna drive her home? 'Cuz we ain't releasing her car 'til we take pictures. She parked it a far cry away, with even more of her paintings piled up in there."

I was getting tired of the sound of his smug voice right around this time, so I tried to end our little *tête-à-tête*: "I'll do whatever she wants, I guess. Is she coming out now?"

The sheriff nodded, the Ripo Lake Deputy unlocked a door, and Emma emerged looking equally embarrassed and exhausted. I tried to defuse the moment and smiled.

"Hi."

"Hey."

Sheriff Janssen handed her a black backpack. "Your bag with your two paintings. Say, is that the way they do art out there in Fargo? Hope that's not your best stuff."

A dark cloud passed over Emma's physiognomy as she calmly took her bag. It looked as if she was going to snap and say something, but Emma merely turned away, numbly resigned to her fate. I put my arm around her shoulders and walked her out to my car.

"What the hell were you thinking?" was the first thing I could muster as we drove away.

"It's not what it looks like."

"It looks like you were sneaking around Dutton's property in the night!"

"Well... OK then, I *did do that*," she admitted, "but I wasn't stealing anything. I was just looking. He's burying his sculptures in the ground and in the walls of the studio! What the hell is he doing, Adam?"

At this point, my still half-asleep, cranky mind sort of seized up in a fury. There was too much information, and I needed it all in the proper order, so I let out a bottomless breath, and started at the top: "OK, first of all, why did you have your paintings with you?"

Emma looked down, ashamed. "I...I actually planned to try to go inside. I had a student ID card I was going to use for the lock. And then if I was caught, I was going to use the paintings as my alibi, saying I was retrieving them because I needed them for a sale."

"Emma, what is with this obsession of yours? All the questions you're always asking me about the James family, all these weird, confrontational visits to Dutton's studio? What are you trying to accomplish or learn?"

All at once, Emma exploded: "It's because it *doesn't make sense!* None of it! Why are they hiding his sculptures? Is he planting them? Do they grow into beanstalks? Why does he live in fricking poverty, all alone, in squalor? How can he even cope, let alone create this ground-breaking work? *What's with his dad?* Is he some monster? Why did their family move out to the sticks in, of all places, Contented Cow, Minnesota? Did you know there was a huge fire in the studio's building before they came? The building still looks charred in some places! And what is that chemical he's using? And lastly, I can't even come to grips yet with meeting Dutton James *and* his best friend on the first day I go to Northfield! How did that happen? It's like I'm being Punk'd or something! And now, Dutton's career is just magically *taking off!* Just skyrocketing in front of our eyes, just..." Emma half-heartedly made Dutton-like fireworks noises.

I rubbed my eyes as I drove. "OK...anything else you need to know?"

"Yeah! Did you *even know* that Dutton's big showing is tomorrow night? In New York City?" I nodded. "Why isn't he there? He told you he was going to the Twin Cities with his sister?!" Emma stared out the window and exhaled hot breath onto it. "It's like something led my life to this place and time for a reason. Some purpose. But I don't understand any of it. And all I'm getting is more and more confused."

A light rain started to fall. I turned on the wipers and commenced answering her bevy of queries: "OK, first of all, Dutton *wants* to live alone. He's told me that many times. He's very proud of it. If his bedroom isn't clean or well-kept, well, that's just him. He's always been covered in a thin film of dirt ever since I first met him in the second grade. And I brought up the exhibit in New York to Dutton a few days ago, and he acted like it didn't even matter to him. He laughs it off or tells you you're lying and that it's 'just art' and 'who cares?'!"

"I know…"

"And to be honest," I went on, "I'd probably be more upset if he *was* attending his exhibit because that would mean they brought him there to exploit him and make fun of him! 'Hey, look at the weird dude who made the amazing art! Isn't he hilarious?' Let's face it, nothing Dutton says ever illustrates or illuminates the subject of his art anyway. He doesn't seem to either know or remember how he does it at all! He just does it! So since he's unable to discuss his methods, he'd be a pretty poor interview for the New York art critics anyway, wouldn't he? No, the more he's kept out of the spotlight, the better."

"By the way, did you ever find out what that pebble from his sculpture is made of?" Emma asked.

I shrugged. "I gave it to a science guy. Nothing yet. As far as Dutton's dad goes, yeah, he's a jerk. And then two of his wives died, and now he's even more of a jerk. He used to be poison in this town. But he and Dutton talk on the phone, and he visits every few months, give or take, so he can't be all that bad! And as far as the fire, that was before Willow James was even in that studio! It was some kind of Native American trading post then, and there was a fire, and then I assume Willow James refurbished it because she probably got it for a song at that point! Look, you can ask me anything. I'll probably know it. I could maybe even talk Dutton into letting you visit him again sometime. But please stop this stalking and sneaking around their studio! Now, is there anything else you need to know?"

"Yeah," she said. "Why are they called the Carleton College 'Carls'? Could they be more unoriginal?"

I sighed and launched into my next dissertation: "All Minnesota small college names are a tribute to unoriginality. There's the Saint Thomas Tommies, the Saint John's Johnnies, the Hamline Hammies, the Saint Benedict Bennies and the Gustavus Gusties (and yeah, that's all a real thing). Of course, Sant Olaf, the other college in Northfield, surely had the dignity to rise above this silly naming pattern, right? Nope, they're the Olies. Plus, in Minnesota, the term "olie" refers to a heavily accented, Minnesota bumpkin. So Saint Olaf's Olies are akin to Notre Dame's Fighting Irish, or Washington's Redskins. It's borderline xenophobic or whatever today's 'woke' vernacular is." I pulled into my parking spot and turned off the car. "End of tour."

"Sorry I asked," Emma said, then she suddenly looked around. "Wait. Where are we? Aren't you driving me home?" I gaped at her and laughed.

"You want me to drive to Fargo, North Dakota at five a.m.? You have seriously, *seriously* got to be kidding. I am going back to sleep. You can either hang out on campus for awhile, or sleep on my couch, but

I'm guessing you don't have money for either a hotel room or a bus to Fargo, right?" Emma shrugged. "Do you have anything pressing where you need to get back home right away?" Again, a shrug. "OK then. So let's just cool it for a little while. Hang out a bit, OK?" Emma somewhat sheepishly agreed.

We went to my flat above the Northfield Five and Dime (no this isn't a flashback to the 1930s, that's still the store's name), past the flyers posted along the musty stairway: local rock band gigs, school plays, and the reservation's, showing dozens of their missing kids. Once inside, I made up my small couch for her. She looked at it doubtfully.

"Y'know," she said, "if you offered to take the couch, I wouldn't be at all offended to take your bed."

"Yeah, that's nice of you, but I wouldn't want you to think I was any more of a pushover, seeing as our first three meetings have all revolved around *me giving*, and *you taking* and always expecting more, more, more." I posed like a hammy drama queen, then smiled at her and winked, and she did that thing where she looked me over for seemingly the first time. Emma was funny like that. Then she shrugged, lay down on the couch, and pulled the blanket over her.

"Hey, Codependent Ultra-Giving Boy, come here." Emma motioned me over with a soft smile. I sat down on the side of the couch, my pulse rate quickening just a bit as the blood started flowing. She clasped her hands behind my head, and pulled me down, and kissed me. I didn't resist. After a long, slow kiss (that seemed to last at least a few minutes), she suddenly made a frustrated "ugh" sound, playfully pushed me away, and turned around to face the back of the couch. "You can hold me while I sleep," she said, "But nothing fresh." Yeah, she used the word, "fresh" while rebuffing my lovemaking advances before catching twenty winks above the village Five and Dime. So twenty-three skidoo, I guess it was a real old-school morning. I lay down and hugged her from behind, snuggling into her hair. It smelled amazing.

Nothing "fresh" occurred as we slept in 'til past eleven a.m., when we both seemed to stir out of our sleep at the same time and look at each other. She had a cute, early morning "pooky face." She apparently didn't mind my morning appearance either, since she moved toward me and gently kissed my lips again. Wow. Clearly, no nocturnal regrets developed over the kiss that happened last night. After awhile, her body started grinding up against mine, like an erotic, involuntary dance, and all of a sudden she started tearing my shirt off. When the unbuttoning took too long, I helped out while she ripped her own shirt off.

I couldn't help thinking: *It is at moments like this, right before something is definitely about to happen for the first time with someone I really like, when I like to pause and relish the fact that there is nowhere else in the world I would rather be than right here, right now.*

Suffice to say, things got supremely fresh after that.

Then, in the afterglow, with both of us panting and moaning, "Oh my God... h my God..." over and over so much it made us giggle, we fell asleep until two p.m. I remember somehow I was conscious of being happy while I slept, and I felt somehow complete. I didn't even care that my spine was severed in multiple places from trying to stay on-board the couch all night, unconsciously and desperately clutching onto her for dear life.

When I awakened, however, I had the sofa to myself. Had she left? I squinted around the room through sleepy, puffy eyelids. Something looked different. On the wall above the couch was a painting. It was Emma's! A landscape of trees, with bold, almost Van Gogh-like strokes and swirls. It was really impressive!

"Hey, this is really good!" I was finally able to focus on an Emma-like figure, sitting naked on a wooden milk crate which contained my vinyl record albums.

Wow. She looked really good with no clothes on. As my eyes zeroed in on her better, it became evident that she was reading old issues of the *Northfield News*, which I kept in another milk crate against the wall. I used to be a reporter there for the princely sum of twenty-five dollars per week, and I had kept all the issues that featured my contributions.

Only something else was off. I stretched my lids open with my fingertips to gain some clarity, and I saw Emma's face was, to coin a phrase, stunned-wide-open as she read the paper, i.e. her eyes were bulging wide, her mouth ajar, her nostrils flaring, and for all I know her pores were gaping open as well. Hers, though, was an expression not of horror, but of a sort of astonishment mixed with pleasure.

"Hey, what's up?" I said. "You're an amazing painter! Do I get to keep that?"

She looked over at me with the same, mind-boggled look of impressed shock and awe, as if I had just told her that I had gone back in time and killed baby Hitler, and she actually believed me.

"Wow," I said. "That must have been some article I wrote that week. Was it my hard-hitting exposé on cow-tipping?"

Emma tossed the newspaper on the floor with the others she'd perused, and sat on top of me, all the while holding that same, mind-addled expression.

"Adam Winters. You are just full of surprises, aren't you?"

"What the flip did you read? Oh! Was it the first review *ever* of a Dutton James sculpt—?" I never finished the sentence because of Emma's immediate need for freshness. *Man*, I thought to myself, *it took over twenty years, but I was right: That reporter job with the Northfield News was a total babe-magnet.*

I never did remember to ask her what she was reading that day.

Sheriff Janssen

Hours later, the sheriff knocked on the door, and Adam opened it.

"Hello, Mr. Winters," Sheriff Janssen said, smirking. Although it was dusk, Adam still appeared supremely exhausted. "Long night?"

"Very funny," said Adam.

"Well, after you picked her up at the police station, I saw your car parked here only minutes later. Mind if I come in?" he asked. Adam glared at the sheriff and leaned back against the doorjamb.

"Not unless you've got a warrant," said Adam sullenly. The sheriff seemed taken aback at Adam's rebellious chutzpah. "Wow," Adam continued, "This here is some Big Government we've got in little Northfield, doncha think? Almost colossal! No, you can't come in, Sheriff. Why are you here?"

"Ain't no reason to get snippy. Ain't hard to see your car parked from Water Street, is it?"

"The fricking nanny-state in action. Kinda surprising, since your ilk seem to be against this type of big-government overreach. Can I ask your political affiliation, Sheriff?"

"No, you may not, Mr. Smartass. That's not relevant to anything."

Adam winked. "Make Northfield Great Again, huh? How long have you been sheriff here? Sixty years or something? Isn't there a mandatory retirement age in this country, or is that more of a state thing?"

The sheriff smelled the air. "What's that smell? Something I should be concerned about?"

Adam pulled his door closed and resumed leaning, but even a sheriff with sunglasses on could mark Adam's gargantuan effort to appear calm while he silently trembled with rage. "I've got a license for medical marijuana use," said Adam, flatly. "'Course, you must know that since you recently seem hell-bent on sticking your nose in my business..."

"OK, watch it, mister..."

"Why don't you check my records on your computer for the umpteenth time, and you'll see I have chronic headaches from playing football, hence the legal, medicinal odor."

"Oh, believe me, I remember you playing football," taunted the sheriff, "Because them who don't remember the past are forced to repeat it! Right?" The sheriff cackled, "Who said that?"

"Santayana, and I gotta say, I'm surprised and impressed you know that," said Adam, actually pretty surprised and impressed. "Yeah, you seem very fond of razzing me in public about your hazy memories of one damn football game. Don't ever hear you mentioning the fact that I was first team All-State for four years. What happened, Sheriff, you lose a bet on that championship game or something?"

"Hey, watch it there, Winters!"

"Not good enough that I gave my body and brain and risked everything for you and your fanatical, pathetic high school football cronies? I left my sweat and blood all over the place for all of you. What's the matter, not good enough unless I die for the cause?"

"Yeah, well, I remember the condition you were in when you arrived for that championship game—"

"Yeah, so you've been telling everyone for twenty years! I was in pain. My mom just died so I had no parents, Sheriff. I was managing it the best I could."

"That what you called those bottles of booze? Pain management?"

"You're only as good as your last game, huh, Sheriff? That's the way people think who've never played a goddamn sport in their life, you ever notice that?"

"Alright, wait a minute, buddy-boy—"

"Oh that's right, I forgot. You go bowling every week, doncha? Damn. It's impressive you even remember the rules with your senile gray matter—"

Suddenly Sheriff Janssen's arm shot out and pinned Adam's neck against the wall. Janssen's mouth and entire face were shaking. "You better watch your tongue, boy."

"What the—?"

"You ever hear that song by Bobby Fuller? 'I Fought the Law'?" asked the sheriff, "I wouldn't recommend it, pencil neck."

His face a deep beet red with the sheriff's forearm compressed across his throat and all, Adam Winters stubbornly grinned, slowly crossed his arms, and choked out the words, "The Clash's version was better..."

The sheriff studied Adam's obstinate, madly-grinning visage and then released him, as if he saw all at once what he was doing.

"Just watch your mouth, Winters."

"What are you gonna do, Sheriff? Shoot me? Why the hell are you even here, other than to harass a law-abiding citizen?"

"I came to tell you about your little red-headed girl, Charlie Brown. The Native Americans want to press charges. Trespassing. She here? I need to bring her in."

"Oh, please. She's just a friend of Dutton's and a fan of his art. And no, she's not here, she took a bus home hours ago."

"That so? Well, we looked at her record. Miss Thing's had a lot of run-ins with the law."

Adam laughed. "Really? In that hotbed of crime, Fargo, North Dakota? Oh yeah, I forgot: That Coen Brothers' movie *Fargo* was based entirely on Emma. The FX show too."

"No, smart-guy," said the sheriff, "in Chicago over the last buncha years. For vagrancy, illegal drug use, loitering..."

"Oh please, what, you mean like protesting?"

"...breaking and entering..." Janssen went on, "...attempted theft of art..." Adam blanched at that, and the sheriff noted it and pounced. "Oh, you didn't know about that, did ya?"

Adam sneered at Janssen. "What the hell are you talking about?"

"At the Art Institute of Chicago," said Sheriff Janssen. "Last year. She and her hippy friends tried to steal a painting. And take a wild guess whose painting it was?"

Adam shrugged. "I dunno. Her own?"

"Nope. Willow James."

"What?"

Sheriff Julius Janssen's lips curled up, finally satisfied. "Yep. Look it up yourself. It was in *The Chicago Tribune* even."

Adam shook his head. "I will look it up. 'Cuz I don't believe it."

"You'll see. What did you call her? A fan of Dutton's art? Yeah, that's one way of putting it. She's an art thief, boy! And apparently, she has a particular affinity for the artwork made by the James family. I personally believe she was trying to steal Dutton's sculptures!"

"Oh, she was not."

"Yeah, I'm sure Miss Emily's got you believin' whatever she wants by now. Damned carmine-haired deviant." The sheriff's already snarled mouth raised up high into a nasty sneer, revealing a mouthful of crooked teeth that matched the general shade of Spongebob. "Hey, Winters," he said, "by the way, do those rosy-red carpets of hers match the drapes?"

Adam squinted at him with loathing. "You're unfit for your office. You're unfit to work at this town's Tastee Freeze. And you need to step down, Sheriff, before something really bad happens to you. Forever tarnishes your spotless record."

The sheriff put his face an inch away from Adam's. Adam could smell his breath. Cigars and garlic.

"Is that a threat? Boy?"

Adam doggedly grinned. "Nope. Merely an observation."

"Well, I got an observation too. If your little carrot-top chicky-doodle steps foot in this town again, I'm gonna take her in. And that's a promise. You hear me?"

"Yeah," Adam said as he pulled away. "Have a good day, Sheriff Janssen."

"I'm enjoying this day already, Citizen Winters." Adam soberly closed the door behind him. "Did you get all that down?"

Mrs. Mayhew's voice emerged from down the stairs. "Most of it."

"Thank you, Janice."

While Adam stormed across his apartment to check the internet for information on Dutton's exhibit that night and possible past criminal activity on the part of Emily Astrid Kincaide, the sheriff waddled down the stairs and out the door onto the Northfield sidewalks.

Dan Auerbach

Dressed in a $230,000 tuxedo, the Silver Jackal smiled as vaguely as the Mona Lisa while floating his way around the Perriman Gallery, located at 72nd and Madison, in the heart of Manhattan's art scene. It was at times like this when Dan felt there was literally nowhere else in the world he'd rather be. He was the Undisputed King of New York today, at least at this particular, annoyingly-fleeting moment in time.

Everyone there seemed breathless, trying to find words to intellectually describe Dutton's art, some mansplaining the machismo found within the artist's chiseled strokes, while others womansplained Dutton James' clear feminine bent, and how refreshing it was to see such an uncluttered mind that was so unafraid to explore his own misogyny.

"I mean, it was almost like those celestial-forms were raising their tentacles and saying, 'Me Too'!"

"I saw that too. I'll bet you anything he binges all day on fish oil and estrogen..."

The gallery had been a carnival of luminaries. It was to be an unceasing all-day, all-night affair, a breathtaking celebration of the new, mysterious, rising superstar, Dutton James.

"*Did you know he's Willow James' son?*"

"*And did you know he has Tourette's or autism or one of those conditions?*"

"*His brain was damaged in an accident, and then he started doing art. Like he was struck by a creative thunderbolt!*"

"*Please. He body-swapped with Willow James' ghost, was what it was.*"

Normally, in a gallery like this, there would be lulls throughout the day, ten minutes every now and then when no one was present because, after all, no reservations were ever required. (What better way to achieve the absolute maximum number of people?) So, judging by the laws of large crowd behaviorism alone, one would expect occasional dips in attendance. Today though, it never fluctuated to less than a hundred visitors at any given time; Daniel Auerbach knew this for certain because he counted them.

Dan took a deep breath. He was never comfortable with small talk and glad-handing, and even less so as the years steadily wore on. He was seventy-eight now. He had to conserve his energy and never let on that he was doing it. All the same, Dan smiled and met hundreds, maybe even thousands of people that week. Had he met them before? Who knew? Probably. That's why Dan always knew to keep his greetings vague (*Say "Good to see you", never add the word "again," and never, ever say "Nice to meet you"*).

The lone Jackal looked around at the high-ceilinged, cavernous room, the largest of the five in the gallery, all filled with Dutton's art. The sculptures had suggested opening-bid prices listed beneath the pieces' descriptions, and the last thing Dan did before they opened the doors to the public was raise all the suggested bid tags twenty percent from their already gaudy sticker prices. He did this for many, many reasons, too numerous to count (although it would be fair to say they all included the end result being *more money*), but the biggest reason Dan did it was because he felt it in his gut. Now, admittedly, even Dan knew his "gut" was nothing more than a bunch of collective, visceral feelings mixed with a smattering of objectively-biased hunches, but it was also the most important thing Dan Auerbach possessed in the world, acquired over years as an art agent, and none of the younger art peddlers could match it. Maya Slotky, at age fifty-something, was within spitting distance of being Dan's heir apparent if she kept working hard... And something about Maya's demeanor this time around seemed to show that she finally, at long last, recognized Dan's brilliance, unblinkingly doing whatever Dan demanded of her, including having to, at the last minute, change every sculpture's meticulously printed opening-bid prices to reflect Dan's any whim. *Was it a know-your-place power play, changing all the prices?* Dan smiled. *Probably*, he thought.

He glanced over at Maya whose spider senses must have been tingling because she was already looking back at Dan. As per usual, Maya was juggling five conversations while checking the room in anticipation for the next five. This time, however, she was also patiently waiting to get Dan's attention. Having received it, Maya raised her eyebrows questioningly at him and tilted her head towards the small stage next to her.

Dan looked down at his watch. It said eight p.m. EST. He smiled, shrugged, and nodded to her. Maya adroitly sewed up her myriad discourses with The Met, the Guggenheim, and Sue Forbes and William H. H. Forrest from the Walker while gracefully ascending the stairs to the microphone, and then seamlessly speaking into it: "Hello everyone, and welcome, welcome, welcome to this extraordinary event we have all been so lucky to be a part of!"

The audience had already begun applauding, half of them with excitement, the other half anticipating her voice's obviously building modulation, knowing a pandering applause line in the making when they heard one. Maya thrust her crystal wine glass in the air and shouted, "Thank you! Thanks to all of you!" As the clapping reduced to a smattering, she continued, "So I'm not going to be long. You all know the auction will commence tomorrow, Saturday evening at seven p.m., at Sotheby's on York Avenue. Hopefully you've already cleared up and liquidated a goodly amount of money in preparation because, folks, the estimated value of these wondrous and indescribably superb sculptures by Dutton James is literally rising by the *day*—not month, not year, but by the day—as is illustrated by looking at your programs! They were printed two days ago, and the prices listed in there are already nothing but a fantasy at this point! We simply can't keep up with the escalating worth of these pieces! And although Dutton couldn't be here, we have the next best thing, which is his agent and father. *Ladies and gentlemen, Mr. Dan Auerbach!*"

Another round of cheering began as Dan ascended the stairs (giving Maya a debonair peck on the cheek) and settled in at the microphone, nodding, and waiting for this rush of love and appreciation to end. He smiled, bemused at this human, biological need to willingly offer their collective submission to him in the form of ridiculously slapping their hands together. So silly. *But then again, it was all for the legendary Dan Auerbach, so do go on,* he thought.

Dan tried to look embarrassed and humbled, laughing and motioning for the cessation of clapping, but on the inside he was eating it up. Ever since he was a child, this was all he had ever craved. Attention. And then when Dan met Willow, he realized how he could successfully achieve it. *And then,* after laying his eyes on his son Dutton's offerings, Dan was able to envision his final act, the impetus for this swelling, warm orgy of appreciation.

The applause died down and Dan spoke.

"Thank you so much. I just first want to say that Dutton is so sorry he couldn't be here, but as of a few days ago, he fell ill, and he couldn't make it."

A small murmur went through the crowd as Dan went on. "And not wanting to be specific about his ailment, I just want to wish Dutton my love, my thoughts, and our hopes and prayers that he get better...because this time, I don't mind telling you, I'm a little worried about him."

The audience's murmuring morphed into an all-out buzz, though muffled, in a dignified manner, which was only proper.

"After all," Dan went on, "first and foremost, we must all be concerned about his health, not the supposed value of this artwork if, God forbid, the Lord chose to reclaim his tortured soul from the earth in any sort of untimely way. I love you, Dutton, get better," Dan Auerbach said to absolutely no one, sending emptiness into the ether, knowing full well Dutton was not watching, nor listening, since he was with his sister, Lily.

Dan sighed nostalgically. "When I was young, in Southie, and that's a tough part of Boston, we never had any money. I was taught by my parents to value, maybe even overvalue, the almighty dollar. Money and all the various creature comforts that accompany it were something to be earned. And appreciated. Never taken for granted. I grew older and attempted to become a young artist, although I wasn't very good..." (There was a brief sampling of amusement from the crowd, and Dan smiled sheepishly.) "I was never gifted by the gods with artistic talent. But then I met Willow James, and I saw the possibilities of true genius. And luckily for me, she allowed me to be a part of that, to let me put her on the map, and join her as a partner in learning about the world of great art and the many ways to invest...in beauty! And I learned that it wasn't so much about money, but it was more helping to *create and spread beauty* that mattered. And then after she...bore our last child...whose name is Dutton...I lost her."

Here, Dan knew he needed to pause. His seventy-eight years had certainly taught him to read a room better than most. With some "difficulty," he went on. "I thought we'd lost everything we had of Willow! Her spark, her..." Dan paused even longer this time, as if he was remembering Willow, when truth be told, he didn't remember much about her at all, other than what was in their photo albums, coupled with the fact that she seemed to always be gone, in the studio, working.

Dan went on. "But then we discovered more of her paintings, and while it yielded great monetary gains, what is *more important*... is that it made the earth and its inhabitants just a little more whole and just a bit closer to God. And then after Dutton's unfortunate incident, and after my second wife, Linda, died in a car accident...I thought that was it. I assumed that our limited little family unit had nothing left to offer the world anymore, and maybe we should just take it easy for a little while, and just appreciate the time we have, together, while we have it. Just my son, Dutton, my daughter Lily, and myself." Another long pause. Then Dan looked up, looking new and transformed. "And then a miracle happened. I don't know if Dutton's unfortunate accident somehow... conditioned his brain to receive beauty, or something...but *it seemed as if the spirit of Willow started growing in Dutton*. Right away, we could see it... He just... sprouted a great knack for art and sculpture! For the first time! And although it was raw, I helped develop and nurture it. And I believe Willow thinks this too, wherever she is now, that *what you see here today, in these rooms, all these unbelievable works of art, this is the new gift that Willow James has offered to the world through her son, Dutton.*"

Thunderous clapping grew into a standing ovation which died down quickly as they sensed Dan was very moved and needed their support to go on with his speech. "I feel that everything you see here..." Dan went on, "...will be the lion's share of Dutton's gift. That the spirit of Willow seems...less strong...recently..."

Somewhere in the crowd, the tiniest smile washed over Maya's face before it faded behind her mask of melancholy as she thought, *The Silver Jackal, in his element. So slimy, yet so brilliant. He's doing precisely the same thing he did with Willow. Find a mentally unstable, borderline feeble artist, then oh, so subtly exaggerate their health issues and as a result, their life expectancy, and watch the art's value rise, and watch Dan get rich.*

The Silver Jackal went on. "But if this is all Dutton is able to give, I say it is enough. It is *more* than enough. His body of work is as large already as many of the world's great sculptors, and...I just hope Dutton learns to lay his demons to rest, to let them sleep." (Appropriate pause.) "So please. Don't merely think of all this as only a great investment. Which it is, there's no doubt about that. Think of how you... who are *lovers of real ART...*" Dan grimaced intensely, making fists, his body shaking with passion. (It was the "climax" of his speech) "...Think of how *you* can better this world by controlling just a little bit of its *beauty*. And how important that is. Because if this is all we're going to see out of Dutton James, these fifty-odd sculptures, and if this is the end of the legendary James family circle and cycle of art, then we should be touched, and humbled, and grateful that we all got to be a little part of it. Remember this when you bid on these pieces tomorrow. How awe-inspiring it is to get a chance to truly possess and control something...that *contains a little piece of God.* I ask you, how do you put a man-made value on *that*?"

He tearily beamed and surveyed the room. Then Dan Auerbach smiled bravely and finished.

"Thank you."

Maya

Maya's heart beat like an AK-47 in her fire engine red dress.

"We have one million-five. That's one million-five. Anyone for one million-five? One million-five."

"Six." The softly spoken bid sounded as if weakly surrendering, almost semi-whining "Okay fine, whatever..."

"We have six. One million-six. One million-six. It's now one million-six. Anybody? One million-six? One million-six? Any—"

"Seven." The reliable, steady, bass timbre of the item's most frequent bidder, a middle-aged, Harvey Weinstein-looking, portly man with an obnoxious New York accent, who not only seemed to guide, but to produce, direct and dictate the pace of bidding on this item, the penultimate art piece of the night, *Drip Study 2*. His style of bidding was to sound bored. Like he was forever intoning, *"Hey, I can keep doing this all night..."*

The other bidder, who looked like a seventy-year-old Julia Roberts, looked doubtfully at her husband, an eighty-year-old Jason Sudeikis. Then, together, they visibly contracted into their seats, simultaneously diminished as if they had just voluntarily expelled their twenty-one grams of life force.

Seeing this, the auctioneer knew he had a clear winner, and he hurried his cadence: "And we have one-seven. Do I hear one-eight? One-eight? One-eight? And—" He loudly banged the gavel. "Sold to number 142 for the price of one million and seven hundred thousand pounds!"

Maya couldn't help but wince at every mention of the British monetary denomination that Dan Auerbach had insisted on for the auction's bidding. *How utterly pretentious! We are in New York, bidding on the work of an artist from Minnesota, and here's Dan the Gouge insisting the auction's bids must be presented in British Sterling?* Maya smirked as she walked down the center red carpet, flanked by the two-hundred-and-seventy chosen bidders, seated on either side. *In addition*, she thought, *not only was it faux-elegant, but everyone knew the grift.* American bidders considered the dollar as overly-strong versus the struggling pound. The last bidder had bid 1.7 million pounds (probably thinking that was equal to around two million US), but he actually now owes more like 2.2 million-plus US dollars. Dan was making a killing. The good news: this also meant Maya was making a killing.

Maya breezed by the seated Sue Forbes and William H.H. Forrest from the Walker Art Center (proud winners of three pieces of Dutton's at an average of 800K each) and arriving at the side of Weinstein's-slightly-less-repellent-doppelganger, nudged him in the shoulder, and whispered in his ear, "Nice one,

Jamie. Let's hope you've still got something left now for the *piece de resistance*."

Maya turned and strode back toward her preferred position, along the wall near the exit. She was fully aware how her flaming red cocktail dress hugged her still-cute figure just right, so when she walked she gave her smart, tight ass just enough swivel to give the impression its perfumed anus was whispering, "*Yep, tough* and *sexy.*"

Maya was surprised to find herself genuinely smiling, for *real*, for the first time in longer than she could remember. Because it was almost over. She glanced quickly at Kira, standing at the opposite wall, and did a small double-take at the way Kira was already staring back at her. It wasn't just that Kira was visibly admiring Maya. That was commonplace, considering Kira's cloying codependency that shackled Maya to her. It was the *way* she was looking at her. Sort of with an evil, leering twinkle. Like she wanted to get hate-screwed or something.

Maya shot Kira a quick smile, took a deep breath, and looked up at the ceiling trying to imagine if there were something, *anything* she would rather do *less* than have sex with Kira again. Meanwhile, the other auctioneer, the female one, approached the stage as the gathering radiated a low, excited hum.

Nope, thought Maya. *I can't think of anything.* Still, she knew she'd probably have to schtup Kira at least a few times more before retiring to Maya Island with Rachel McAdams. Because Kira could be useful for one or two more chores. Dangerous chores. And then, if things went to plan, Maya wouldn't even have to endure the messy breakup or the ever-churning Manhattan Rumor Mill because it would all be Kira's doing: The whole breakup, and the whole amicable monetary settlement (*"The outcome that was so remarkably generous to that 'Kira girl,'"* they'd all say, *"who hung around Maya those last few years, but she was never anything but a tall surrogate dildo for Maya Slotky."* That's all they'd say. And that, Maya could handle).

The auctioneer banged her gavel. "I have the final item up for bid tonight. Can we reveal it, please?"

She backed away from the microphone so everyone could get a look at what was widely believed to be Dutton's greatest work, *The Demon Lady* by Dutton James.

The lights softened as the velvet curtains opened along the back wall to reveal one of the most startling works of art that Maya had seen in her thirty years in the business.

It was lit from within the piece, mostly pointing up from underneath, revealing a seven-foot-tall, majestic yet unnerving manifestation of some kind of unearthly Demogorgon spider, stretching scores of appendages through its glassy casing and emerging outside of its clear shell, as if thrusting itself out at its witnesses, both beseeching them for help while attacking in a violent blur.

Maya couldn't prevent her need to involuntarily inhale oxygen into her lungs at the sight of it, and it caught in her throat as if she were sobbing, so awesomely grand was the sight, and so staggeringly, shockingly, fabulously lofty was the amount of money she was going to make from it. By her calculations, she had already cleared more than 8.7 million dollars for herself on the night. Now this could push her closer to an even ten mill. Not even in her wildest dreams could she have imagined earning that much tonight.

The crowd emitted a sort of stunned, gasping exclamation, and the excitement of that sweet sound washed over Maya, making her eyes well up with tears. This was her *peak*. And this was also her *swan song*. The crowning achievement of her entire, hard-earned life's work. What more could anyone ask? She was fricking Michael Jordan. Going out on top. A living legend.

"This is universally regarded as Dutton James' finest work of art. *Demon Lady*, named after his mother, the artist Willow James, the so-called 'Demon Lady of New England.' Here, Dutton James pays tribute to his legendary matriarch, almost a companion piece with his mother's famous painting of the same title, yet striking in how different it is from its namesake. It is as if Dutton James brought her painting into our real-life dimension, yet still, it somehow appears *more than 3-dimensional*. It boasts an almost holographic feel yet remains completely ensconced in nature."

As the auctioneer recited the description of Dutton's James' *Demon Lady*, Maya couldn't help but feel that her remaining time in this world wasn't for long.

That life, it seemed, was oh, so fleeting. That she must, to paraphrase the poet, *gather her rosebuds while she may*. She had to appreciate and enjoy the little time she had left.

Because Maya knew in her soul that the James family was cursed.

Willow, Dutton, Lily, and Dan, all of them, tragically cursed.

And ever since Maya became a willing participant in the James family's sphere, merging with their maleficent, grey-black aura, she had become cursed as well. *And* Kira. *As was* Kira's unfortunate *predecessor*, Marie-Ann, sweet Marie, who died of cancer almost a decade ago.

(*And* Dan's dead second wife, who Maya Slotky secretly had killed because of her gouging practices.)

They were, all of them, *all of us*, cursed by the legend of the *true* Demon Lady, the tortured spirit known as Willow James.

After all, it was the Demon Lady herself who once told Maya that she *knew* the James family was cursed.

That was the day before Willow James committed suicide.

And now, this same curse was attached to all the money Maya was earning tonight.

"We are going to start the bidding at 2.7 million pounds."

All of it was *cursed*.

ACT II

So shall you hear
         Of carnal, bloody, and unnatural acts,

Of accidental judgments, casual slaughters,
Of deaths put on by cunning and forced cause,
    And, in this upshot, purposes mistook
    Fall'n on the inventors' heads: all this can I
    Truly deliver.
    Let us haste to hear it,
    And call the noblest to the audience.

From William Shakespeare's play, *Hamlet*

CHAPTER 1 (January and February)

Dutton

I hide them where the fire was. In the walls. Nobody ever look here. It no big deal. It just art. It like garbage from a stupid truck.

My dad tell me it OK. But he say to never tell anyone else.

And he say *no more art now! Keep art a secret!* We make more money when we don't make so much art!

So I say I get rid of some of it. I sell it at fairs and in my store.

Then Dad come here with jerky lady Maya. I called her Mayo. She laugh but I have a secret too 'cuz I hate mayonnaises. I like ketchup. I even put ketchup on a art once but Dad just wash it off.

Dad and Maya give me bank check for fifty-thousand dollars 'cuz they had a secret auction! I don't believe it! I rich now! I going to finish fences like dad said, and I buying lots of ice cream.

I can't dig easy 'cuz the ground froze now. But my dad tell me to hide them so I try more. And I tell Dad I going to destroy everything 'cuz there's no more hiding places. Dad get *really really really mad then and he yelling don't destroy it! Don't destroy them!*

There are shiny blinky Christmas lights outside, but Christmas was a hundred days ago or something.

Then the old police guy from Northfield knocking loud on the back door. He yelling my name a lot. So I hide so he won't see me. So he hit at the door and it fall down and lots of bright pretty lights are in my eyes. He saw me.

"Dutton, time to come out now," he say. "What the hell are you doing? What the Sam Hell is going on in here?"

"I hiding things. It no big deal, it just art."

"Dutton James, I need to bring you in for questioning." Then he say quiet and closer, "C'mon, Dutton, let's go. There's a new way of doing things now. Looks like you're not being protected no more."

"No my dad say you protect me! He give you money to protect me—"

The old guy stop me talking fast. "Now, Dutton, you know that's not true! Stop that! Jason, you might as well read him his rights. Just to be safe."

Then the young police guy start talking like *Law*

and Order. "You have the right to remain silent..."

I say, "No, you protect the Jameses! My dad pay the Johnson police guy!" The Johnson man put his scratchy hand on my mouth hard.

The Jason police guy keep talking. "Anything you say may be used against you in a court of law..."

The old policeman Johnson whisper to my ear. "C'mon, Dutton. Things are different now. Let's get you in a nice warm cell and get you some hot chocolate."

Then I say you have hot chocolate? and he says yes, so I go with him while the Jason guy kept talking about what is right or something.

I cold anyway. The police car is warm when I get in. I tired of living in cold houses. The genny broke now anyway. I freezing. I go have hot chocolate with Johnson and Jason police guys.

Emma

"I seriously can-not *believe* this has all been *happening*, and I haven't done anything *about* it!" I excoriated myself while I groggily prepared for bed during this winter's 10,000th giant blizzard. "But I won't bring it up to Adam now," I rebutted myself, "because I can't."

Not until I find out more about what's going on.

Adam said he still hadn't received word from the Carleton science department, but I sort of doubt he had even been trying. He had something inside of him that needed to protect Dutton, and I honestly doubted if he was ever going to help me at all. *I've only seen Adam a few times, after all, and now it's even more difficult ever since that geriatric policeman told Adam he would arrest me if I went down to Northfield again.*

I was absolutely stunned two weeks ago to see Dutton James' picture on the cover of none other than fricking *Time* magazine with the caption, "artism." He was smiling a Dutton smile, messy hair, super-imposed over one of his *insane-looking* sculptures I'd never seen. The article was on up-and-coming artists, but it also had an insert article about autism and the successful use of art therapy to soothe their troubled minds (at least that's one thing that makes sense about Dutton being an artist). Temple Grandin talked about how spectrum autism helped her envision pictures to draw her ideas, and how autism forces one to be fixated on needs or desires, which can help in the creation of great art. *Sounds a little like me*, I thought, *other than the "great art" part.* It also mentioned that Michelangelo was rumored to have had autism, possibly explaining his obsessive fixation on taking four years to finish the Sistine Chapel. Any way you sliced it, ever since Dutton's auction, which was among the highest grossing in history, Dutton James was on top of the art world.

Weeks ago, while surfing Dutton's glowing reviews, I tried to Google what I saw in that issue of the *Northfield News* at Adam's flat, and I actually found it on the internets, and I saved it to Photos on my phone. The issue was July 7, 1997. Page seventeen.

And the photo of interest didn't even accompany one of Adam's stories. It was a black-and-white picture of a crowd of people, gathered on a football field at night, watching fireworks.

There were no names listed underneath the photo, just the photographer's name with the caption, *"Northfield residents celebrate the 4th of July in style at Knight's field!"* (Why they felt the need to include that exclamation point at the end of the caption, I'm not sure. I figured it was just the way papers wrote things before I was born, like in old *Life* or *Look!* magazines or something.)

But it wasn't the caption that caught my attention. It was a face in the crowd.

And the face was of a young Adam Winters.

There was no doubt it was him. Younger, darker, more compact, sure, but there he was, in his varsity football jacket, amid a crowd of people standing and looking up at fireworks.

Many more people were below Adam, reclining on their blankets and pointing at the sky, and they were presumably the central image of the photo. Yet, if you really studied it, you could make out the blurry Adam in the upper right portion of the picture.

However, when I first saw the photo in Adam's apartment, it wasn't Adam that drew my attention. It was *someone else*.

It was Willow James. She was well-hidden behind someone's head, but it was her, alright. Who else in town could have grown that bold grey hair, with streaks of black? But she wasn't looking up at the sky with everybody else. She was looking straight ahead.

Having an insatiable urge to see the picture again (and noting that, even though we were currently experiencing the winter's 10,087th power outage, my phone was at 89% so it was worth wasting the juice), I sat on my bed and found the old black-and-white photo I had saved. See, if you really scrutinized the pointillist photo dots, and if you, in addition, possessed the capability of modern phones to zoom in, you could see it.

Willow and Adam were touching hands.

Secretly.

It could be seen by studying the crowd's legs. Their two hands were touching, below the masses, while everyone's attention was pointed skyward. He was standing behind her, looking up at the sky. She was looking forward, as if making sure no one saw.

I found the photo and zoomed in as closely as I could. And that's how you could make out Adam's other hand.

It was resting on Willow's ass. Clear as day. And sure, some could argue, *What does this prove? Maybe they brushed against each other at that very moment.* To this, I would instruct the prude naysayer to note their body language. It was utterly relaxed. Completely in sync with one another. Comfortably touching each other the way lovers do.

And since then, I knew. And by now, I'd known for weeks. But like I said, *I can't ask him about it.* Because Adam wasn't telling me the truth about things. And if I was going to learn anything about what was really going on in Northfield, then and now, I had to act as if I didn't know anything.

In other words, I had to pretend I didn't know that Willow James once had an affair with her hometown's star high school quarterback, Adam Winters.

As I settled into my cold bed, the power came back, and as the bed lamp and digital alarm clock burst on, I noticed a blinking phone message on Grandma's landline answering machine I hadn't noticed before. (Yes, not only did she still have an answering machine, but it was probably the first one ever made, being the approximate size and weight of a curling stone. Grandma said she bought it used, and there was an old message already on it of Alexander Graham Bell testing it out by reading "Mary had a little Lamb." When I was a kid I believed that story. Now I see it was probably a joke, huh?)

I pressed the giant PLAY button, and after four eternally long underwater beeps and then another forty-five seconds of scratchy silence, I heard Adam's warbly voice, sounding like he was radioing in from an antique biplane over Berlin.

"Hi, Emma. And Grandma. It's Adam. The results came back from the Carleton lab. The most interesting finding is that Dutton's sculptures are made of many things, including a whole lot of DNA."

Staticky pause.

"Human. DNA. And sort of a lot of uh...plasma and blood."

Another long silence hissed loudly from the machine, broken intermittently by Adam's distorted, soft breathing. "So that. I'll just talk to you tomorrow. It's late, and I'm tired, and the power's out over here, so what the hell, may as well sleep. Bye."

I must have sat there with my mouth gaping open in astonishment for five minutes after hearing that. *Human DNA and blood were found in the sculptures of Dutton James? What the hell does that mean?* I reset my blinking alarm clock with a six-a.m. wakeup and snuggled further into my three layers of rapidly warming electric comforters with all of this racing through my mind.

I must have fallen asleep because the next thing I remember was being awakened by the alarm's loud buzz, and then before I knew it, I was holding a black thermos of coffee (steaming up my car windows) as I stupidly drove to Northfield to confront Adam about Willow, while testing my confrontational words out loud: "Why didn't you tell me? How long were you together? Was it just a tryst? Because I sure as hell know *something* happened!"

Then, of course—because what else would happen to me?—five minutes into Northfield, right after the cows and contentment sign, a black-and-white started following me, and as soon as I parked at Adam's, he turned on his flashing lights, and one of Northfield's finest got out of the cop-car and asked me if I was Emily Kincaide. I said, "Yeah," and quick as a wink, he was restraining my hands and driving me to the station so that I could verbally wrestle with the decrepit, half-wit, part-sheriff, part-mentally-deranged-grizzly they keep there.

What I didn't know then: Early that morning, Dutton James had also been taken into the Northfield Police Station, and everything had already started to unravel.

As I rode in the back of the pine-smelling police car through the "frozen tundra" (a redundant misnomer if there ever was one), I tried to comprehend what Adam's phone message could mean. *Dutton's sculptures were partially made with human blood.* It was hard to imagine any good coming from that.

Maybe, I slowly realized, *Willow is..."in" Dutton's sculptures. Literally. Willow's body was never found, after all,* I reminded me, and then quickly banished this notion and admonished myself: *Look, Ems, either Willow James previously fabricated her own work to pass off as Dutton's before she died, or that's her, chopped up inside his sculptures, but you've got to choose a conspiracy theory and stick with it, for cracker's sake.*

I wondered if the human blood and DNA finding explained why Dutton was already at the police station when I arrived, but no one ever seemed able to tell me why he was brought in. All the police kept saying was that they were keeping him under house arrest because of a possible flight risk, and that he was to be arraigned tomorrow at the Northfield courthouse.

In the meantime, I couldn't stop obsessing over the secret I discovered on my own. And it was as plain as the pussy hat currently perched on my frazzled, red noggin of hair.

Willow James and Adam Winters were lovers.

Adam

A serious-looking man at the Northfield Police Department bolted up to me and grabbed my arm, saying, "Adam Winters? Come with me. I want to ask you some questions." I shrugged "sure" and followed him into a room.

[Later, I saw our discussion was in the court transcript, so it's included here for accuracy's sake.]

"State your name for the record first, please."

"OK, so yeah, I, Adam Winters, actually did that. I procrastinated for awhile, and I wasn't even sure I was going to do it, but then, yes, we did it. Joshua Larkin and I. We did it."

"Who's he?"

"Joshua Larkin? He works in the Laird building at Carleton College. What's today? Wednesday? He's probably there now. But don't bug him or anything because it was all my idea."

[INTO PHONE] "Yeah, get me a Joshua Larkin. He's in the Laird building on the Carleton campus. Get him here yesterday."

"OK, why are you doing that? Look, admittedly, I was the one who started it all. We're both on the faculty ultimate frisbee team, even though I'm in administration, and that's not faculty technically, but they let me play anyway. Because I'm, like, pretty good. I was on the Carleton ultimate frisbee National Championship team! Once upon a time. Against Division 1 and everything! How 'bout that?"

"So tell me what happened then? Joshua Larkin did the test for you?"

"Yeah! He, Dutton, well, he had nothing to do with it. I just obtained a little pebble from one of his sculptures. He sells them in his little store for like twenty bucks or whatever. So I got a pebble to see what it was made of, you know? Dutton is always so secretive about his art and everything, I just was curious. And maybe I was a bit worried, too, that he was using some kind of chemical that was dangerous or he couldn't handle. Like, you know, maybe something was left over from the Willow James Studio days or whatever. So I went to Joshua, my, my frisbee friend in the science building."

"Emily Kincaide didn't ask you to do this?"

"What, Emma? Did Emma ask me to check out Dutton's art? No. Like I said, I was just curious. So I said to myself, I said, 'This art thing is a mystery, and I should check this out.'"

"OK."

"So I went to see Josh and asked if it was even possible. To test the pebble. And Josh said yeah, he could do it. I never even told him it was from Dutton's sculptures. I just said I found it and couldn't place what it was, so could he do me a favor, and I'd pay him if he wanted. Are you going to answer that?"

[INTO PHONE] "Hello? He's there? Yes, bring him in. Five minutes. OK. Mr. Larkin is coming here now."

"Josh?"

"Yes. He's going to join us. Any objections?"

"What? No. I'm just surprised. It's kind of embarrassing, I guess."

"Anything you want to tell me before he comes in?"

"Like what?"

"Like his findings."

"His findings from when he tested the sculpture stuff? A lot of long chemical names which I frankly haven't had a chance to look up yet. Look, I came here to see Dutton because I heard he was, like, arrested for something, and they say I can't see him, but I'm almost like his guardian here, in a way. This town is poison for him. His dad and sister don't live nearby, and he's all alone, so I try to look after him, I always have. I should be allowed to see him. Does he even have a lawyer?"

"I'm not allowed to speak about Mr. James right now."

"Well, isn't that what we're doing? Speaking about him?"

"Yes. We currently have Emily Kincaide here for questioning as well. You know her, right?"

"Of course! She's here? Why?"

"She said it was her idea to get the sculpture piece

tested, and she asked you to do it. Is that correct?"

[7 SECONDS OF SILENCE]

"OK. Yes."

"Why didn't you tell me that before?"

"I don't know. Just. Didn't want to get her involved. Who are you, anyway?"

"She's very involved, Adam. It says here you signed her out from the Ripo Lake police station after she was brought in for attempted breaking and entering at Dutton James' art studio."

"It wasn't breaking and entering. It was just trespassing."

"Yes, and now she is being charged for that incident. That was her intent, though, to break-in, wasn't it?"

"No! Absolutely not! She's just a friend and a fan of his. That's all. She's being arrested now?"

"The Native American reservation is pressing charges on her now, yes."

"The Northfield Police told me they'd arrest her if she ever came into town again, and I relayed that to her! So she never came back!"

"I didn't bring her in."

"And who are you again?"

"I'm not with the Northfield Police Department. Before we finish, is there anything else you want to tell me? Before Mr. Larkin joins us? About his findings."

[10-SECOND SILENCE]

"Blood and human DNA."

"I beg your pardon?"

"In Dutton's sculptures. They found human DNA. I found out a week ago. And I procrastinated because, I don't know, I had to think about it. But I did tell the FBI. I called them and spoke to an Agent Bailey. Because I was worried."

[INTO PHONE] "Hello? Who? OK. Adam, you're going to have to excuse me for a moment."

"Where are you going? You can't hold me here! Who are you?"

"Sir, my name is Special Agent John Bailey with the FBI. Excuse me, please."

"You're Agent John Bailey? Why didn't you tell me? You're the one I talked to on the phone, right? Hello?"

[AGENT EXITS. 20-SECOND SILENCE. AGENT REENTERS]

"Mr. Larkin, I believe you know Adam Winters."

"Hi, Josh."

"Dude, what is this?"

"And this is Sheriff Julius Janssen of the Northfield Police Department. Please sit down, Mr. Larkin."

"Dude, what is this?"

"Sorry, Josh."

"Does everybody here know each other? Sheriff?"

"Oh, Mr. Winters and I are very well acquainted, aren't we, Adam?"

Sheriff Janssen

When Sheriff Julius Janssen looked out the window and saw the small gaggle of three or four local reporters setting up outside his police department building, he knew this was a situation he needed to get in front of, so to speak. "I should go out there and talk to them," he said.

"Yes, sir," answered Mrs. Mayhew.

A plainly dressed, dark-haired, suit-and-tie guy in his early thirties approached the sheriff. He looked like a Fed. "What are you, FBI?" asked the sheriff, just then noticing Adam Winters at the station's front desk, gesturing angrily at the desk sergeant. "Dagcrappit, what the hell is the Winters boy doin here?" the sheriff demanded in his severe, exquisitely-Minnesotan tone.

"Probably asking into Dutton," replied Mrs. Mayhew (whose inflection, modulation and twang was every bit as Minnesotan as his, by the way). Here, the plain-dressed Fed tried to interject while he recognized a small window.

"Yes, Sheriff, I'm Agent John Bailey, FBI."

"Well, what the heck are *you* doin' here?" asked Mrs. Mayhew.

"Mrs. Mayhew, please!" grunted Janssen. "Listen, Bailey? You cannot talk to Dutton James until we are done with him. This ain't your case."

"Not yet. Did you just say "Winters is here"? Is that Adam Winters or his son?

"He don't have any kids..." proffered Mrs. Mayhew.

Agent Bailey frowned. "Oh, well, he just called him the 'Winters boy,' so—"

"He calls anybody under the age of 100 'boy,'" said Janice Mayhew. "I'm pretty sure it's a power thing."

"*Oh, it is not,*" whined the sheriff. "*And will you shut it?* Look, Mr. Man, you're welcome to ask Adam Winters any questions you like. He ain't involved in this. In the meantime, I gotta talk to the press." Sheriff Janssen then mumbled at Mrs. Mayhew, "You should come with and stand behind me. Just look real serious and professional, you understand me? Don't make faces."

"When do I ever make faces?" protested Mrs. Mayhew.

"Constantly," growled the sheriff as he pushed open the front doors and waddled regally toward the reporters, who were already shouting questions at him. Janssen held up his hands to quiet them.

"Hello, I am Sheriff Julius Janssen. That is J-A-N-double-S-E-N. This morning, at approximately one a.m., we brought in the well-known artist, Dutton James, and held him for questioning. We have not officially charged him with anything as of yet, and I couldn't tell you for sure if an arrest is even imminent. What I can tell you is that Mr. James is being questioned, and he is fine, and that's all I can say. In the meantime, this is a whole lotta nuthin'." The reporters yelled questions again, and the sheriff barked above the clamor. "We would appreciate it if you would move aside now, and let us get on with our business—Janice, let's get Jason out here to rope off an area for the reporters— and if anything of substance occurs, I will let you know. Thank you." And with that, he and Mrs. Mayhew walked stiffly away.

Once back inside, the sheriff walked into his office and turned up the volume on a TV monitor showing a black-and-white split-screen of the station's three interrogation rooms; Dutton James sat in one, Emma Kincaide was in another, and Agent Bailey's interrogation of Adam Winters was in the third. "We should have a one-way mirror installed in the interrogation rooms," the sheriff groused. "Write that down, Janice."

"Where in ever-loving tarnation are we going to find the budget for that?"

"Just write it down."

"When would we ever need a one-way mirror except for right now—?"

"Now, exactly, right now..." mumbled Janssen. "Shh. What did he just ask him?" demanded the sheriff, pointing at the monitor.

"I don't know. *You were talking—*"

"Shh."

On the monitor, Adam Winters looked up at the

Fed agent and said the words, "Blood and human DNA."

The sheriff's eyes bugged out, and he turned to Mrs. Mayhew. "What in galloping Jehoshaphat did he just say?"

"Blood and human DNA," repeated Mrs. Mayhew.

A voice called into his office. "Sheriff, Joshua Larkin is here. They're saying the FBI agent wants him."

"Alright, I'll be out in a second!" Staring at the image on the TV, Janssen picked up the phone, pressed a button, and the phone rang in the interrogation room on the monitor. The Fed picked it up.

"Hello, Bailey, we got Joshua Larkin in the building now, and we're coming in," said the sheriff.

"Who is this?" asked Bailey on the TV.

"This is Sheriff goddamn Janssen, and we're coming in!"

The sheriff hung up, charged out of his office, and spied a nerdy-looking white guy in his twenties with messy, tangled hair. "You Joshua Larkin?"

The man looked up and blinked behind bifocal lenses. "Yeah, uh, sorry, can you tell me what this is about?"

"No I cannot. Come with me," snarled Janssen as he grabbed Larkin's arm and marched him down the hall. The federal agent was just emerging from the interrogation room.

"Sheriff Janssen," said Agent Bailey, "I'd like to ask Mr. Larkin some questions in private to corroborate their stories before—"

"The hell you are," barked Janssen. "Did Adam Winters just say there was human DNA in Dutton's artwork? Well, anything involving Dutton James involves me. C'mon. Let's go."

"Dude, let go of my arm. What the hell is going on?" demanded Larkin.

Agent Bailey opened the door and the three spilled into the room. "Mr. Larkin, I believe you know Adam Winters."

"Hi, Josh," said Adam, sheepishly.

Larkin looked dumbfounded. "Dude, what is this?"

"And this is Sheriff Janssen of the Northfield Police Department. Please sit down, Mr. Larkin."

Larkin sat down in a chair next to Adam and glared at him. "Dude, what *is this?*"

Adam winced and shrugged. "Sorry, Josh."

"Does everybody know each other here? Sheriff?"

Janssen took off his tinted prescription sunglasses. "Oh, Mr. Winters and I are very well acquainted, aren't we, Adam?"

"Hello, Sheriff," said Adam, matching the sheriff's glare and mirroring it back at him.

"Did I just hear what I thought I did?" Janssen asked Adam incredulously, "Did you just say that those sculptures contain—"

"If we could just interrupt you, Sheriff," said Bailey, quickly laying his hand on Janssen's old paw, "I'd first like to ask Mr. Larkin a question: Joshua, what were your results pertaining to the chemical makeup of the object Adam Winters asked you to test?"

Larkin frowned and looked at Adam. "What, that glassy-looking pebble you gave me?" Adam nodded. "Uh, let's see there was polychromicsorbitate. There were elements of zinc and uh... sulfuric acid, elements of clay, and some plasma and DNA."

"What kind of plasma and DNA?" shot back the sheriff.

"Definitely not animal. We were ninety-eight percent certain it was human DNA," said Josh.

"And how much of it was *in there*, may I ask?" inquired the sheriff.

"Well, we took only a few tiny samples of each of the various areas of the object so I couldn't say for sure. I remember one sample contained a lot of it, I think. Maybe seventy-five percent."

Janssen waddled to the door. "Will you excuse me, please? Carry on."

The sheriff shut the door and charged down the hall. He stopped at another door and opened it. Emma was sitting alone at a table, and as the door banged open, she jumped.

"Jesus!"

"Young lady," intoned the sheriff, "Did Adam Winters ever tell you what they found in that piece of Dutton's sculpture?"

Emma looked confused. "Adam? Why? Is he here?"

Sheriff Janssen stared, trying to decide what he could and couldn't say. "He is here. Maybe you two should meet and get your story straight."

"What story? What the hell are you talking about?"

"*Did he tell you?*"

Emma sighed. "Yes, he said it contained DNA. He left a message on our answering machine."

"And you didn't think to *tell me that* when I questioned you?"

Emma shrugged. "You never asked about it."

"Excuse me," said Janssen, quickly shutting the door on her and barreling down the hallway. "Janice, you here?"

"Like always."

"Get me a hot chocolate, would ya?" Mrs. Mayhew sprang into view from a dying-ficus-plant camouflage and walked in the opposite direction. The sheriff paused outside another door and took a breath, trying to settle his thoughts. He then slowly turned the doorknob and peered inside, smiling. "Hey, buddy, how you doin'?"

Dutton James sat in a dingy, grey, windowless room, handcuffed to a table. He looked tired, scared, and even a little dirtier than he usually did. He recoiled when the door opened and looked at the sheriff, confused, squinting up into the room's bright fluorescent lights, his face a mask of horror and grief. "Wha is happening, Mr. Johnson? Wha is happening? Why I here? I don't know any girl! I don't know that girl!"

Janssen nodded at the officer standing guard. "Jason, you need to go-ahead and rope off an area for those reporters outside, wouldya?" The officer nodded and exited, closing the door.

Sheriff Julius Meriweather "Wampum" Janssen slowly lowered his self down next to his prisoner and rested his textured hand on Dutton's. "How you doing, Dutton? You want another hot chocolate?"

Dutton rolled his eyes and shrugged. "OK..." Before the sheriff could speak, Dutton interrupted him. "Who Jan?"

The sheriff blinked dumbly at Dutton as if he had just spoken Mandarin. "Hujan? Oh, "Who's Jan?" Janice Mayhew? My assistant? She, uhh, well, she works here, see, and she helps us out with police work."

"She your mother?"

The sheriff blinked again as if his mind was rebooting. "Is Janice Torkelsson-Mayhew my mother? Well, no, Dutton. No, she's not."

"Then why does everybody keep calling you her son?" asked Dutton. "They keep saying, "Jan's son, come here! Jan's son, go do this, Jan's son go do that." Why they do that?"

The sheriff frowned at Dutton, his eyes ever-so-gradually laying bare his growing comprehension, and then, abruptly, he burst out wheezing and laughing. Mostly wheezing.

Dutton had never seen the old policeman smile or laugh before. Wrinkles spread over the old man's eyes and cheeks in a scary way, like his face was being clawed from behind, and he was laughing about it. "You be careful 'cuz I tink your face is breaking," said

Dutton, and Julius Janssen jovially wheezed again, laughing, pitching forward, his face a burgundy red. "I tink your head exploding or something. What's da matter? You embarrass she your mother? It OK."

The sheriff rubbed his eyes, his laughter subsiding. "Jan's son, he says! That's rich. That's a good one, Dutton, that really is."

"It OK! Just say it! Cuz *I* am "*Willow's son*", so maybe people call *me* that sometime *too*..."

"No, Dutton, my name is Janssen. Not 'Jan's son'! Sheriff Janssen! Dutton, you and me have lived in this town for your whole life! You mean to tell me you still don't know my name?"

Dutton shrugged and looked down, ashamed of what he was about to say: "My mom always say I remember people names if I like them. I don't remember names if I don't like people." (The sheriff absorbed Dutton' not-so-veiled insult.) "I remember Adam's name! He my friend! And Emma's name! She pretty." Dutton frowned. "Where my hot chocolate?"

"Janice!" The sheriff bellowed.

Mrs. Mayhew immediately entered the room and placed a Styrofoam cup in front of Dutton, mumbling something about "Cocoa getting cold...", then to the sheriff: "You, my "*son*"? *I'm only forty-six years old... You must be a hundred-and-fifty*, you old buzzard..."

Janssen barked back at her, "I told you not to listen at the door, Janice."

"Then how would I do my job?" her muffled voice came as the door shut. The sheriff shook his head.

"Funny. Always thought she in her mid-sixties..." Dutton drank the hot chocolate in one gulp. "Damn, boy, you're hungry, aincha?"

"I thirsty. Can I have watah?"

"You want some water? Sure! But listen, Dutton, I gotta ask you a question. I just heard somethin' a little weird. *What is it* you put in those sculptures of yours?"

Dutton promptly became agitated. "Why you ask me this? It just art! Why I here? I don't ever touch any girl! I don't know her name! Why you say you can't protect me no more? You call my dad?"

"I'm going to, Dutton, but we've got reporters here, we've got the FBI, and *they all need to know how you make those sculptures, Dutton.* They *all* need to know *now*."

Dutton looked staggered by these revelations about the FBI and the press, traumatized, *horrified*. His expression altered as if a great disturbance had passed through him, and he struggled to speak, stuttering nonsensically.

The sheriff seemed distracted, then stood up and put his ear to the wall. "Just one second, Dutton," he said, while charging through the door, into the hall, and yanking open the next door over: "What the hell is going on in here?"

[According to camera recordings, the exact words that the sheriff probably heard before interrupting the conversation between Agent John Bailey and Emma Kincaide was Agent Bailey saying the words:

"So maybe we can get some coffee and discuss—"]

"Hey! I should be present and/or witnessing any and all interrogations here!" yelled the sheriff.

"Sheriff Janssen, we should speak in private," answered Bailey.

"Right here's just fine," stated Janssen.

"OK," said Agent Bailey. "Emily Kincaide was just admitting to me that she knew about the blood findings from the sculptures. Did *you* know anything about this before today?"

"Of course not!" bristled Janssen, shutting the door behind him. "And what the hell are you suggesting? Dutton James is some murderer or something?"

Emma shook her head. "I can't believe that. There's *no way*. I mean, I've even read that some of Willow's paintings contained *her* DNA because she included her own menstrual blood!"

Agent Bailey shook his head. "It wasn't Dutton's DNA we found in there."

"What are you talking about?" yelled the sheriff, "That boy Larkin just said the DNA's identity doesn't show up on the chemical test! That you gotta do a different test!"

Bailey nodded. "And the FBI did. We obtained multiple sculpture pebbles from Dutton James' little shop."

"Then *whose DNA is in them?*"

"Not just one person. There were multiple findings," said Bailey.

"I beg your pardon?" asked the sheriff. "*What does*

that mean?"

Bailey shrugged. "I'm not at liberty to say."

"What are you saying, now he's some kind of serial killer?" raved Janssen, "Give me a break!"

Emma shook her head again. "No way."

"So *you knew* about this blood-and-DNA thing before you came today?" the sheriff asked Bailey. "Why are you even here, Agent Bailey? I certainly never asked you to come."

"We got a phone tip from Adam Winters about finding blood in Dutton's sculptures a week ago. Because of the subject's high public profile and renown, we checked it out and rushed a DNA test through. Our findings were, without prevarication, disturbing. At that time, it became the FBI's case."

"I was never told—"

"Then we discovered the Northfield police were in the process of arresting Dutton James and Emily Kincaide early this morning," Bailey went on. "Since they are both subjects in our investigation, I came down to see what the hell was going on. And I must admit, I still don't know why you brought either of them in here, Sheriff Janssen."

"*She* was brought in for trespassing at the James ArtStudio!" insisted the sheriff. "And Dutton is here because—*now this is a delicate subject, now*—Dutton is here because a young lady from the Indian reservation accused him of improperly touching her, and that's all I can tell you because of anonymity issues and whatnot. Now, maybe we got our facts mixed up, but then that's why he's here, ain't it? For 'questioning'! To figure this all out! Here, maybe we should be talking privately, Agent Bailey."

"That's why I suggested it five minutes ago," Bailey said flatly, and laying his personal card on the table in front of Emma. "Keep it." He smiled. "Let's talk."

Once in the hallway, Janssen shut the door and pivoted angrily to Bailey. "I told you that you could not interrogate either Dutton James or Miss Kincaide without me."

"This case is now jurisdiction of the FBI, Sheriff," said Bailey.

"Now, why would the Feds be interested in a little case like this? Ain't nothin' even been *proven yet!* What the hell did you find along with that human blood anyway?"

Agent John Bailey looked up, deciding if he was going to actually share, with Sheriff Boob here, classified information. At this juncture, he figured he may as well: "Look, there was such a wide variety of DNA results, it raised some flags. So we visited Dutton's art studio this morning, after you brought him in. We wanted to look around to see what we had."

"You *what?* You had a warrant for that, I presume?" asked the sheriff.

"Didn't need one. Didn't need anything at all," said Bailey.

"If you even stepped *one foot* on—"

"Didn't even need to. See, we're standing on the side of Dutton James' property, surveying this junky back yard, looking over the patches of half dirt, half weedy grass, with all kinds of rusty paint cans half-covered in snow, and we're wondering if this special-needs kid, Dutton—"

"He's not a kid," whispered the sheriff.

"...does he *have it in him* to gain access to *human blood* as a medium for his artwork? And why would he? He'd purchased some corrosive chemicals on the credit card that his dad manages, and that certainly interested us—"

"Uh huh..."

"...but there were no medical purchases of plasma or anything of that nature," said Bailey. "So then our canine runs onto the property—"

"Without the proper warrant you cannot enter...-"

"First of all, that's debatable," Bailey said. "Secondly, we *have* the warrant, and we will obtain a judge's *signature* on our warrant..." (He checked his watch.) "...in approximately twenty minutes from now. Thirdly," concluded Bailey, "I told you we didn't enter the property. I never said our *dog* didn't mistakenly get away from us, did I?"

"...Mm hm..."

"So the damn dog takes off on us," says Bailey, smiling at the memory, "and we're discussing the studio building, and the doors and windows and so forth, and Blue comes running back to us carrying a big stick—"

"Blue's the dog?"

"Yes, and Blue's a *young trainee*. Gets overly-excited sometimes, wants to play fetch in the middle of an investigation...*not good, right?*" Agent Bailey said, laughing, "Not good..."

"No, not good, no."

"So I take the stick, and then I just immediately drop it on the ground because I recognize the type of stick this is."

"What kind of wood?"

"And Blue starts going after it again, and we say, 'Blue! Heel!' And Blue just stops and sits right up like a cadet! He may be a young one, but he knows what to do when we tell him to heel, you know what I mean?"

"Uh huh..."

"And I look down at the stick. And it's exactly the type of stick I thought it was."

"What, a, a paint-stirring stick, or...?"

"The stick was a human femur," said Bailey.

The sheriff had a slightly senior moment when he heard this because, at first, his face remained blank for a few full seconds. Then he laughed as if he didn't understand a joke he was just told. Finally, it seemed to "hit him" when he frowned, suddenly perplexed, and took a step back as if someone had just pushed him. "A what did you say?" asked the sheriff.

"A human femur. It's actually the largest bone in the human body."

Somehow, it seemed as if the entire police station had just then become silent. No talking, no yelling, nothing. It was just one of those coincidental interludes, or hiati, in the office. Still, a tad awkward...

Janssen grabbed Agent Bailey politely by the shoulders, pushed him tactfully down the hall into his office, and slammed the door.

"*What did you just say?*" asked the sheriff.

"A human femur."

"And have you tested...?"

"We are, yes. But it was only this morning, so, no results as of yet."

The sheriff gently guided Bailey into his chair and pointed a finger down into his face. "I am going to continue questioning Dutton James now. You can watch it on the monitor here."

"You don't have a two-way-mirrored interrogation room?"

Agitated, the sheriff said, "You hear that, Mrs. Mayhew...?"

"Budget, Julius..." came her voice from the darkest of corner of the office. Then: "I thought they were called one-way mirrors."

"Same meaning," explained Agent Bailey. "It's stupid, I know."

"Alright, fine, Bailey," Janssen conceded, "I'll be accommodating to you just so long as you remember that it's gonna be reciprocal when the case is yours. Got it? So I *will* allow you in the interrogation room, but you will *not* say a word until I see this warrant in now-seventeen minutes, which is only based on your say-so anyway."

The door opened a crack: "Sheriff, the Dutton boy is yelling and throwing a fit. He looks bad."

Sheriff Janssen burst out of the door followed by Agent Bailey, and they entered Interrogation Room Three to find Dutton in the throes of some kind of a seizure. His hands and fingers strained against the handcuffs.

"I want WATAH!"

"Get him some water!" the sheriff yelled through the open doorway to Mrs. Mayhew. "Dutton, this here is, uh, Mr. Bailey..."

"Get me *off the handcuff!*"

"...and actually, Dutton, he's with the FBI," continued the sheriff, quickly getting his keys out to remove the handcuffs.

Dutton became silent, and his pale, grimacing face glared at Bailey (verifying to all that he knew the meaning of the acronym, 'FBI'). "*Watah please!*" The sheriff sat down next to Dutton, fumbling through keys with shaky, old hands.

"That's coming right away, Dutton. *Now listen*: You know what DNA is?" Dutton looked away and shrugged. "Well, now, what that is, is a little piece of a human body. And Dutton? *What would you say if we found some of those pieces of a human being...in those sculptures you do?*"

Dutton gaped at the sheriff, thunderstruck and paralyzed, and steadily growing more and more aghast as he measured bit by bit the meaning of the words. Any blood that Dutton James had remaining in his pallid, sallow face rushed away until his blue lips contorted into a feeble grimace. Dutton tried to speak a final time, but his lips were shaking, and nothing came out. A little drool appeared on his lower lip.

"Dutton, you OK?" asked the sheriff, finally removing one of the cuffs.

But Dutton wasn't there anymore. His eyes rolled into the back of his head, and he began seizing, his hands making groping, clawing gestures as he reached out his one free arm in despair to the sheriff, wretchedly, eagerly straining out at him with panicked, hysterical-looking eyes.

Sheriff Janssen's unfortunate first, knee-jerk reaction was to burst out of his chair in horror to try to get the hell away from the monster that was Dutton James. Then, when Agent Bailey rushed over to help Dutton, Janssen covered up any perceived sissyness by continuing on to the door (as if that's where he was headed to in the first place), flinging it open and yelling, "We need a doctor in here! Right now!"

Mrs. Mayhew peered in the doorway, saw Dutton spasming in the chair, and dropped the bottled water to the floor. The water glugged out onto the carpet, and the sheriff couldn't help but feel bothered by it. A little panicked even. But that was just him in his old age "not able to gauge the level of importance to attach to an event during a string of unexpected occurrences..." (according to the dementia pamphlet he grabbed off the bulletin-board-wall in the empty lobby yesterday.)

"Holy jeez!" exclaimed Mrs. Mayhew as she saw Dutton.

"Alright, just stay in here, Janice!" shouted the sheriff. "Stay with him. I'll be right back!"

The sheriff rushed out the open door, quickly shouldering past the gathering looky-loos, and stormed into his office, shouting as he slammed the door, "We need a doctor in Room Three! Right away now! Call an ambulance!"

As Janssen jerked closed the window shade in his office, he saw, in a flash, a tableau of the entire police station in pandemonium. A mixture of uniforms and reporters rushed by ("Who let the press in? Dammit, Jason!" yelled someone), accompanied by yellow-vested emergency medics pushing a gurney into Room Three's open door and past the chagrinned Mrs. Mayhew who could only gasp and shriek.

Sheriff Janssen turned the volume down on the TV monitor showing the three-way split-screen of Joshua Larkin and Adam Winters still stuck in Interrogation Room One, FBI Agent John Bailey releasing Emma out of Room Two, and then both of them rushing into Room Three, dodging the paramedics who were flooding in to help Dutton.

Sheriff Julius grabbed a cell phone out of a desk drawer, pressed a button on it, sat down...and then stood up again...and then, finally, chose to lean on the desk, his mind a whirling maelstrom. Finally, the ringing in the sheriff's ear ceased.

"Hello, Dan? It's Julius."

Dan Auerbach

Dan Auerbach couldn't believe what he was hearing. How could things have gone so wrong, so quickly? He stood up from his desk and stared down at the harbor, alarmed and agitated, yelling into his phone. "Well, *how is he now?*"

"They're rushing Dutton to the hospital as we speak, Dan. You sure he's not an epileptic? 'Cuz it looked like an epileptic-type seizure to me."

"Goddammit, no! Just... *what the hell happened, Julius?*"

"What *happened?*" asked Janssen indignantly, "I picked him up at one a.m. like you told me to, after you goddamn woke me up, screamin' at me, sayin' Dutton's destroying his new artwork in some such way, and to goddamn *put him in a jail cell until you figure out what you're gonna do with him*, even if I gotta goddamn '*make up a charge*'! *That's* what the hell happened, Danny! So I went and did it! You're welcome. And sure enough, Dutton was defacing a bunch of his sculptures (and he's babblin' somethin about how *you* told him to destroy them, by the by), but *either way, I've got my orders*, so I got him out of there! *And I can't get back in the studio now because it is getting to be a place of intensive interest, Danny."*

"Look, *I'll leave tonight!*" Dan declared, "I'm just worried I'm going to find dozens of sculptures in, in absolute disrepair! I just... *I can't get through to him anymore!* I tell him to stockpile it, and he thinks I'm telling him to destroy it! I can't have him out there either demolishing that art, *Julius*, or hiding my investments where we'll have no way of ever finding them again, *Julius!*"

"*Why don't you get someone out there livin' with him, for chrissakes*, and lookin' after him and such? Lily, or a professional worker, or—"

"*You know why* I can't have anyone seeing what's going on out there! Not even Lily! And *I* certainly can't live out there!" Dan insisted.

"When I got him last night, he was shoutin' outloud things about how you're 'paying me to protect him'—"

Dan hung his head. "No, no, no..."

"And by the way, you gotta start ponying up more for this crap, Dan... So I start askin' Dutton about some woman who was accusing him of improper touching and whatnot, and we needed a statement."

Dan sat down. "Jesus, Janssen!"

"Well, what the hell else am I gonna bring him in for, when he's *in his own private residence at one a.m.?!*," the sheriff hissed, "You said it was a goddamn emergency!"

"Yeah, I know but..." Dan's rubbed his hair nervously. "Jesus, you didn't have to scare him half to death. How is he?"

"They're working on Dutton as we speak, Dan. Now I wanted to pin the improper-touching accusation on this redhead stalker-fan of Dutton's that we caught at his studio a few months ago (she's an out-of-towner), but the boys just brought her in for trespassing, so, she being *here*, I just said it was an anonymous Indian girl that accused Dutton. And that's when the problems started."

"*Then* they started?" yowled Dan.

"Yeah, the redhead starts going on about how she asked a local boy, Winters, here, to check on the chemical makeup of Dutton's sculptures!"

"Who, Alan Winter?"

"The Adam Winters boy, yeah," said the sheriff.

"I remember him," scowled Dan. "He's a putz. I'll talk to him."

"So it's all haywire at this point!" continued the sheriff, "And now this FBI agent wants to question the Winters boy."

"The FBI! Jesus H. Christ!" shouted Dan.

"Yeah, they're here too, Danny! So I give Winters to the FBI to keep them busy while I figure out what to do. And *here's* where it starts getting out of hand."

"*Here*?!"

"Dan? Word somehow leaked that the police had picked up 'the famous artist, Dutton James' or some such, on the AP wire! So now the press knows!"

"What? How could the AP—?"

"I think these local reporters listen in on our radio

so they can ambulance-chase stories and whatnot (I actually know for a fact they do that), and before I know it, there's three or four reporters out here wanting to know what happened, along with the FBI from the St. Paul office, and this Agent-Bailey-guy is saying the FBI's pretty involved now. And here's the worst news of all: They found blood, Dan. Human. In a sample of Dutton's sculptures."

Hearing this news, Dan felt woozy. Like the only bodily position making sense to him at the moment was on the floor, on his knees, forehead flat on the carpet. So his body did this, and he followed. Finally, with the blood rushing back to his head, he spoke from the musty, perfumed shag.

"They what...?"

"And then the FBI, uh...they found a human femur buried in the art studio's back yard."

Dan screeched into the floor, "What in God's name are you talking about!?"

"Well, maybe it turned out better for you. Y'know, in the long run. Know what I mean?" Dan went silent, his mind a jumbled muddle. Janssen clarified: "You wanted to break down Dutton's *immunities*, right? Maybe uh, shorten his life span a bit?" Silence. "I mean, you all but *told me that, point blank*, about a thousand times!"

"*Not like this! You damned ignoramus!*"

"Alright now, let's calm down with the name-calling here..."

Dan rose up slowly from the ground [His office cam

revealed to officials later that he now had an indentation of the carpet on his forehead] and spoke, measured and intense: "We can't have this conversation over the phone. And just let me make it clear for the record that I never told you to harm Dutton, nor did *I* in any way ever *mean to harm him*—"

"Alright, Dan, don't get paranoid. I'm not calling from the Samsung. It's a burner. After this conversation, this phone will be destroyed, and ain't nobody listenin'."

"Jesus, Julius, what could the FBI think if there's human blood in his sculptures? Like he's a fricking killer or something?"

"Well, I don't know about that..."

Dan sat down at his desk and whispered fiercely through clenched teeth, "Julius, this *cannot* go down this way. If it gets out he's some kind of Jeffrey Dahmer type, the value of his art will goddamn *PLUMMET!*"

"Well the problem with that is, the FBI agent already knew about the DNA, and I do believe they are going to seriously look into it."

"You can't let them!" Dan hissed, "Listen, I know a lot of secrets about you, Julius. And I think you know what I'm taking about!"

There was a long silence. When the sheriff spoke, he sounded slow and purposeful. "Well, I guess I could say the same thing about you, too. Couldn't I, Danny?"

Dan Auerbach stood up and furiously paced. "How dare you say that to me!"

"Right back atcha, Danny. And I heard about the damn fortune you made off of Dutton's art. And you are going to start paying me... A LOT more."

Dan stood still and heaved a cleansing, calming sigh...and then he smiled (even though Sheriff Julius couldn't see the Jackal's long, fake choppers, all gleaming white, he could sort of imagine them, hearing the man's voice). "OK, look, forget all that. Let's look at the big picture. Can you minimize this DNA finding to the FBI? Tell them they found blood in Willow's paintings too! Artists do that, put drops of their own sweat and semen or whatever in their art. Convince them to back off this DNA thing. Show them how it's a nothingburger. Can you do that?"

The sheriff sighed. "Well I suppose I could try. Say... You don't think Dutton would be capable of doing anything...*untoward*, do you? Anything...*homicidal?*"

"How should I know what that demented kid of mine is capable of, Julius? For chrissakes! I'm just suggesting some damage control here. And trust me, if you pull this off, you will *absolutely see a sizable bonus in this month's payment.*" (Dan could hear the sheriff's measured breathing.)

"Well, seeing as you brought it up, Dan, maybe you could go ahead and raise up *all* my upcoming payments. You've been pretty damn chintzy, considering the bajillions you made at that last auction of yours. And *you have got to get your ass out here*, brother, and now. I'll phone ya on another burner to tell you where the meet is."

Dan grinned insanely and looked at the ceiling. Of course! He always wanted more money! The true colors of Julius Janssen never failed to be on full, mismatched display, blaring bright and true like an unmuted trumpet bell pointing directly at your face. "Sure, Julius," Dan said calmly. "No problem."

Over the phone, Dan could hear a door open at the sheriff's end, and a female's voice softly spoke in the background:

"Sheriff. We just heard about Dutton James. He arrived at the hospital. He was DOA."

"Jesus, Dan," whispered the sheriff, stunned. "Dutton's dead."

Dan's body jolted, and he dropped the phone and shrunk to the floor again. *This could not be happening.* His hand flailed for the phone, and he brought it back to his ear.

"Get it done," Dan said, growing nauseated, "and ditch that phone."

Dan Auerbach hung up and, feeling queasy, made his way to his private bathroom and vomited violently for the next three minutes before calling to get his private plane off the ground within the next hour.

His son had just died. He had to plan the funeral. Dan Auerbach lay down on the floor, exhausted, and stared up at his office's gothic ceiling, plotting his uncertain future.

After awhile, an expression of serenity tinted his tanned face.

Then, unbelievably (and again, this is known because Dan Auerbach kept two hidden cameras in his office), he raised his fists towards the roof beams in victory.

◆ ◆ ◆

The next morning, Dan parked his rental car at the Northfield Funeral Home in Minnesota and made the arrangements for the laying to rest of Dutton James, who passed away from a massive heart attack the day before. Later that afternoon, after a whirlwind of family and friends and their thoughtsandprayers, Dan arrived right on time at the art studio during a heavy snowfall, parking his rental car as far away from the street as he could manage. The property was now surrounded by orange tape and official-looking signs warning that the property was a crime scene.

Wow, Dan thought, *the FBI moves fast.*

Through the dirty, spotted window of his Lexus, Daniel spied Sheriff Julius Janssen standing off to the back, dusted from the falling snow, outside the cordoned-off lot. He was beneath some poplar trees with a tall man wearing a black hat whose dark tan rivaled only Dan's (although judging by his wrinkles, he probably never moisturized his face like Dan religiously did, and definitely not with any of the expensive creams and oils like the ones Dan owned).

I have to keep my mind focused, thought Dan. What

that one quack doctor told him was "early onset dementia" Dan had decided to self-term "mind-wandering," which was absolutely typical for men his age.

Dan got out of his car into the ten-below-zero chill and remembered to smile sadly at the sheriff and the tall, tan man, even though his mind was filled with anything but thoughts of his newly deceased son. Judging by the tall man's shade and epidermal texture, his tan was neither from a quality bed, nor the preferred, sprayed, persimmon shade/tone commonly seen amongst the rich tradition of the exclusive East Coast ilk which Dan belonged (dubbed MAFIOSAS (Men Above Fifty in Our Successful Atlantic States (Although Dan thought the acronym sounded a little "North Korean," he actually sort of liked the moniker (MAFIOSAS boasted the notorious Trump and his bold epidermoid colorings as the prime, model example of this modern phenomenon (also represented by anybody named Cuomo, and anyone who owned multiple yachts))))). *Whoa. Stop drifting off*, thought Dan as he slowly trudged through the deep snow. Maybe all of this *Sturm und Drang* was taking a toll.

Your son has just died, Dan reminded himself. *This is absolutely perceived to be an utterly tragic event, and people are going to want to see that from you.*

So Dan, wearing his best mask of mourning, traipsed on towards the sheriff and the tall tan man. Dan noted that the men both stood with their arms stiffly crossed, looking out at nothing (obviously speaking to each other in secretive, hushed tones, judging by how unnaturally motionless their mouths were while they both stared robotically ahead). Simpletons.

Dan strode with his hands casually in his pockets, musing that these two were *transparently* members of the Lower 99% (coined by that couple he met at Sandals (*"The 'Upper Ones' are in the House! RUFF! RUFF!"* (That was the line from Snoop Lion at the private 2 Chainz concert at Diddy's he attended (I mean, what the hell? He liked being called "An Upper One," and he hoped it caught on! It makes him feel sort of a *je ne se quois* or... (Dan didn't really know what (It was probably because the words "Upper One" meant lots of money (Dan smiled and shook Julius' hand, thinking, *you two schlubs have no money at all. I win*)))))). But Dan's mind was digressing again. He noted to himself that he must remember to take that pill, made out of jellyfish, to stave off his mind's latterly excessive rot.

And what did all of Dan's described brain "activity" look like to the two men from Southern Minnesota, standing side by side under the snowy poplars? It looked like Dan walked sadly over and shook their hands. And this was very important to Dan. Because being that stealthy was a large key to his success in life.

The sheriff said, "Dan Auerbach? You remember Sam Lightfeather, doncha?"

Dan smiled funereally and used his patented, can't-miss greeting: "Good to see you."

Samuel Flying Lightfeather removed his black hat

and held it by the brim over his chest, looking into Dan's blue-tinted contacts while shaking his hand. It was difficult for Lightfeather to hide his fascination at his own revelation that Dan Auerbach had no idea who he was.

"Yeah, hey Dan. It's Sam," he said with bemused wonderment. "I've rented this land to you for over four decades."

"Yes, Sam, good to see you again. My lawyers take care of all that." (*Where the bejesus could that tan be from? Like, the actual sun or something? (Damn. That would suck.)*)

The sheriff thankfully interrupted Dan's runaway-thoughts process by confiding, "Sam's on our side, Dan, we can talk."

"OK," agreed Dan.

"And listen, I can't tell you how sorry I am about Dutton. I'm just so sorry." Dan wasn't sure if the sheriff was expressing his condolences, or apologizing for inadvertently harassing and terrorizing his disturbed son to death.

"Yeah, me too. My sympathies," nodded Lightfeather with sincerity. Dan nodded and conveyed sadness while not thinking about tans.

"I didn't think it would be cordoned off so soon," said Dan. "I mean, what the hell do they think, Dutton's a murderer or something?"

"Don't think I haven't thought that," admitted Sheriff Janssen, and then staring straight ahead and barely moving his lips, he added in a hushed tone,

"That femur bone could be Willow's, for all we know."

"Oh, stop it, Julius," Dan said dismissively.

"Well, I mean, what the hell is all this anyway, Danny?" asked the sheriff.

"The curse," said Lightfeather.

"What's that, Sam?" asked Janssen.

"The Art Studio. It's on goddamned sacred grounds. This entire reservation is sacred Dakota land. And I knew it. And I took the money and pretended it wasn't so."

There was a stunned silence as Dan and Julius let this sink in. The sheriff spoke first. "Well then, why did you let that Injun trading post put their building up there in the first place?" he asked.

"Because it wasn't a real building! It's still just a tin shack, placed on the ground beside a public roadway, which, by the way, your government built through the middle of our reservation—"

"Gotta stay relevant and roll with the changes, Sammy, they're called asphalt roads..." muttered Janssen.

"—and I let the Linden family *gently use* this small parcel of sacred land because the Lindens were a nice family who were my native American brothers, and they needed the business," insisted Lightfeather. "I did it as a favor, and they did a nice, honest living. And then that fire happens, and the whole family disappears? Didn't make sense, and it still doesn't."

"I didn't find nobody in there!" scowled the sheriff,

suddenly adamant.

"Yeah, I know that's what all of you say," said Samuel Flying Lightfeather, "that nobody died in that fire. Stop saying that! I'm sick of it!" Lightfeather shoved one of his flyers into the hands of the sheriff. "There's kids still missing from my reservation," he said. "Maybe you should be out looking for them. Sheriff." Lightfeather quietly stormed away, leaving the sheriff and Dan standing alone.

"Don't underestimate that guy," said the sheriff. "He was in 'Nam in '72 and '73. One a those reconnaissance, wind-talker solo types, goin' out scoutin' alone with only a knife."

"Damn," said Dan, appreciating Lightfeather's natural tan just a little more.

"I hope nothing happened in that fire that I don't know about," the sheriff mumbled to Dan without moving his lips.

"You tell me. I wasn't there," Dan replied (his lips unmoving also, but only because of the bitter cold).

"Something happened," said the sheriff.

"I don't know what the hell you're talking about," Dan shot back.

"We gotta talk, Danny," said the sheriff.

Maya

Maya shivered in the driving, nearly horizontally falling snow.

She couldn't believe how long she'd been stuck here.

In Minnesota.

In the winter.

Most days, you couldn't even venture outside either the hotel or its tunnels connecting to nearby, indoor portions of Saint Paul. The funeral was delayed for *over two weeks* from its planned date because of a series of snowstorms that laid waste to the states of Minnesota, Wisconsin, and North Dakota. Finally, mercifully, the funeral director announced that the corpse of Dutton James had to be interred very soon, for sanitary reasons and others. Hence, Dutton's funeral was held despite the fact that travel was all but impossible. Still, it seemed like close to a hundred attendees somehow made the pilgrimage to Northfield and shivered along with Maya, Kira, Dan, and Lily. Potentially, there should have been thousands present, with the story of rising star Dutton James' sudden death holding the cable news audience captive for the last few weeks. *Somehow though*, thought Maya, *this impressive-yet-disappointing turnout appropriately reflects the difficult, snakebit, and poisoned life of Dutton James and the rest of his goddamned, cursed family.*

When Maya heard the news about Dutton's untimely death, she was in the process of closing down her studio for good.

Now this changed everything.

She thought she was done with the whole rat race, her money worries finished. So why, then, did Maya feel there was one bit of still-lingering business left? She could have left it alone. But there had always been something *inside* Maya Slotky. Something ruthless. Something that allowed her to rise to the top like curdled cream, and to never be anything less than, at the very least, imminently legendary. And this Something was as much a part of Maya as her arms were, her legs were, and her pretty, fifty-two-year-old, surgically enhanced ass was. Maya just couldn't help but win. Everything. At all costs. Maya involuntarily winced behind the snowfall at the memory of her final fencing championship match, when she mistakenly parried in a pronated first position, rather than a supinated third position, and lost, and then went into such a fury that she blinded her opponent in his left eye with her foil, after he removed his helmet, effectively ending both of their fencing careers. But something in Maya felt she had *no choice. If one had to lose, better to pull the victor down with you.* She was banned from all further competition and never fenced again. A two-time Junior National Champion.

Maya Slotky, *still*, to this day, could not comprehend the concept of losing.

And now, here it was, staring her in her frozen, snow-beaten, tear-stricken face, a way to amass more money than she ever thought possible. She wasn't going to *lose this!*

Maya glanced up at her six-foot-one bodyguard/soon-to-be-ex-girlfriend, Kira, shivering beside her in a faux fur. She could still be helpful.

The pastor mercifully concluded his religious propaganda about where he thought Dutton James was now (Of course, Maya disagreed with his assessment. *Dutton is not in heaven*, she silently disputed, *he's in that coffin, right there*), and the funeral attendees were finally allowed to escape. If anybody at the funeral had been crying, it was impossible to tell since every face was already scarred with frozen tracks of ice as they leaned into the wailing, mewling white squall towards their warm, loving, waiting cars.

As Kira jogged up ahead (*She's so macho*, thought Maya) to warm up the car, Dan stayed behind to speak in hushed tones to a local man he introduced as Adam Winters. *Whoever he is*, thought Maya, *he's aptly named today.*

Maya ruminated on her new, impending fortune to keep herself warm as she trudged forward. Yes, she had her tidy eleven-million-dollar nest egg (10.2 million from the auction, and 800 grand she had managed to squirrel away through the years), but suddenly that amount seemed laughable and quaint to her now. It was as if her entire mind and being, not three weeks ago, before she heard the news of the death of Dutton James, was some long-gone, younger, simpler Maya. So stupid, was that woman back then! So naïve...

Kira hurried around the idling car and heaved open the icy door for Maya, then shut it after Maya sat down in what felt to her like a heavenly, sealed-off refuge. Like a quiet tomb. She closed her eyes and enjoyed the four glorious seconds of silent meditation before the expected *crunch* of the door opening, followed by the never-ending form of Kira Cohn, spilling her gargantuan, faux-furry frame into the driver's seat, and shaking the car like a 6.2 aftershock while she *sker-runked* her door closed again.

She needed Kira. For sure now. One last time.

And then Maya would gloriously emerge as one of the richest women in the world.

CHAPTER 2
(March–May)

E mma

I just couldn't believe what I was seeing and reading.

All over the news, they were talking about Dutton James being a current-day John Wayne Gacy after photos emerged of FBI agents removing bones from the backyard of the James Art Studio. The digging was held up for weeks due to a successful injunction filed by Dutton's father, Daniel Auerbach and his lawyers (rocket-docketed by the local judges they owned), along with the lawyers of the Sioux reservation who were trying to prevent the FBI from "defacing the sacred lands of the Sioux-Dakota tribe reservation." Finally, an agreement was struck, and a judge allowed digging on the immediate property surrounding the metal shanty art-studio building, but there was a stay of investigation *inside the building and outside of the lot* until the courts settled various legal issues on what might be found.

A major newspaper wrote that The Silver Jackal was territorially protecting his famous late son by using his great power and wealth, while most of the blogs said Auerbach was only protecting his investments; i.e. the millions of dollars of potential Dutton James art and Willow James memorabilia which were all reportedly hidden throughout the building and its property. For this reason, the James Art Studio was protected by both FBI agents and Auerbach's own hired men standing guard, 24-7.

This all became, of course, very big news around the nation. Adam received many requests for interviews since he was widely known as Dutton James' oldest and practically only friend, but he refused all of them, as did Dutton's father, Auerbach.

Sheriff Julius Janssen, on the other hand, was on TV more often than catheter ads, constantly spouting his opinions on everything from the investigation ("That femur bone they found was very old. How's Dutton gonna be a mass murderer when he's a baby?"), to art ("To tell ya the truth, there's somethin' about Willow and Dutton James' art that I *just missed*, but you can't argue with the money."), to politics ("We *absolutely* need to make America great once again, Tucker...").

I was contacted by MSNBC for a remote interview about Dutton with Ari Melber, and it was very exciting and all, but when I later saw how I looked and sounded, I refused all further media requests. Not that they were knocking down my door. They probably had a ratings metric that ranked Emma Kincaide a one out of ten on some kind of "good TV" meter, so I imagined I was anathema to them now anyway. I did sell some paintings on eBay and Artic, listed as "Artist Friend of Dutton James" (pathetic, I know). Only forty dollars each, but hey, it's a start.

And then, last week, Dan Auerbach's injunction was overturned, and the FBI initiated digging inside the art studio.

That was when I learned on social media about the FBI's stunning double arrest of none other than Northfield Sheriff Julius Janssen for "attempted multiple homicide," while simultaneously, in Boston, Daniel Orestes Auerbach was arrested "for conspiring to commit multiple homicide." This very morning, the sheriff was to be arraigned in the Twin Cities, although I hadn't heard anything yet.

"Holy Christmas!" was what I wrote when I shared the news feed on Facebook after I first heard, *"Multiple homicides? How could they give us no names, or no more flipping information than that!?"* It got thirteen "likes".

Meanwhile, every day at the James Art Studio, along with scores of Native Americans holding up signs and protesting (and the occasional smattering of woke tourists), FBI agents in dark blue parkas proceeded, persistently digging into April's still-frozen earth inside and around the studio building.

I "visited" the site sometimes (which would simply be me in my antique Civic slowing down to ten mph and peeking as I drove by because, ever since I left the police station with Agent Bailey on the day of Dutton's death, I neither knew whether *I was going to be arrested* at any moment for trespassing four months ago, nor *if I was still banned* from Northfield, Minnesota proper in general). Once I saw Adam Winters speaking near the backyard of the studio to The Silver Jackal himself, just like I saw them speaking at Dutton's funeral. What was up with *that*?

Still. It was time to confront Adam. About a few things. And one of them was that I had recently been secretly dating, unbelievably, I know, Agent John Bailey from the FBI. Just a few times (and only after they dropped me from their investigation), but I sort of thought I should tell Adam, although I didn't relish the chore. Still, I parked at Froggy Bottoms River Pub and Lily PADio on Water Street (my Civic hidden way in the back), walked to the Five and Dime, ran up the stairs, and knocked on his door. It was thirteen degrees below zero, almost a record low for late April in Minnesota, and I already couldn't feel my face.

Adam opened the door and seemed appropriately surprised to see me, considering I'd dropped in unannounced.

"Emma Kincaide! How long has it been?"

"Too long," I said as I pushed past him into his apartment. "We have to talk, Adam."

"I was just leaving—"

"No. Now." Adam shrugged and sat down.

"OK, listen," I said as I started into my prepared presentation. "I've got some things I need to ask you about, and I understand that's unfair because you always complain that I never talk about *my* life *either*, so here goes: My parents decided to just disappear on me when I was young, and then I grew up in a goddamned foster home, OK? So my parents *chose to be just, just, like gone!* They gave me away! And I've always been furious at the world ever since. OK?"

"OK," said Adam. "So then your grandma raised you...?"

"I just call her that. She's not my real grandma. She legally adopted me when I was ten. She was my foster mother. Everyone calls her 'Grandma Fargo' or just 'Grandma,' and now I live there again, *yes, that's right, after I graduated college*, and I pay her rent! OK?"

Adam looked down, sadly. "I'm sorry, Emma, that's too bad. My mom and dad are gone too. My parents both died. My dad of cancer when I was eight, and then my mom raised me in Northfield until she died, tragically, my sophomore year in high school. I moved into a foster home for three months in Faribault until everyone decided that I should just live with my uncle in Northfield. Maybe that's why I always stayed in Northfield after that, even after he passed away. It's like a heroic place to me. Like it saved me from having to go back to that foster home. So I stayed and graduated high school, and then I stayed yet again and went to Carleton College. Graduated in '99."

I couldn't believe I never knew he was a Carleton College grad! *That actually explained so much about him*! I grew suddenly irked that he had waited all this time to tell me, and I erupted at him. "What the *hell*? *I knew it! You're way too intelligent* to be some townie! You're so goddamn *secretive*! Why didn't you ever tell me you went to Carleton, you jerk?"

"Because it's embarrassing. 'Did you go to Carleton? So then what are you still doing here?' It's really hard to explain to people that all I ever wanted was to do was stay in Northfield because...I dunno...I feel some kind of loyalty to it. Or something. Like it's my destiny to stay here, or my duty... So I guess that makes me the hometown boy who went to my hometown college and then stayed in my hometown. In other words, I'm perceived by the world as a total failure because I never left home."

"You had an affair with Willow James."

There. I said it. And the guilt I saw on his face was all I needed to know that it was true. But it was worse. It looked like he was about to cry.

Adam bowed his head. "How did you know?"

"I saw a photo of you two in the *Northfield News*."

Adam shook his head and smiled in disbelief. "God, I know the one you're talking about. That Fourth of July picture, right? I remember we were so nervous anyone would notice when the paper was released. I forgot all about that."

"Why didn't you tell me? What are you hiding from me? Why do I keep seeing you speaking with Dutton's dad? Are you involved in all this James family mystery?"

Adam sighed. "It's always been a secret, Emma, and it needs to stay that way." He rubbed his hair furiously, while thinking. Finally, he said, "Can I trust you?"

I shrugged and nodded. He clearly was in pain.

"The big reason it has to remain secret, Emma, is because it was our affair that started all these chain-reaction dominos of catastrophes within the James family."

"What do you mean?" I asked.

"It was when Dutton was hit by the truck. Willow was supposed to be keeping an eye on him... But she was away because we...we were off...having sex."

"Oh my God," I said. "You can't blame yourself for that, Adam."

"But I do. We were completely mortified and blamed ourselves. It ended the relationship with Willow. And then my mom died soon after that. She killed herself. With pills. She left a note that said she was depressed. And that was that."

"My God..."

"And then Willow...she just checked out. She was despondent. I saw her sitting on her porch, driving by once, and she was just staring out at nothing, face blank. And that was the last time I saw her. Because the next week *she* committed suicide."

Adam covered his face and began to cry. I felt so sorry for him. I sat beside him and said, "Adam, it wasn't your fault."

Adam stood up, wiping his tears away. "C'mon, I

gotta meet Josh. I gotta go."

He put on his coat, and I followed him out the door into the way-below-zero temperatures. As I traipsed behind him, I tried to alter our conversation.

"Do you think Willow was a witch or something? Like a wizard or—"

"She wasn't a wizard," scowled Adam.

"She told people about voices she heard. Voices of the dead. Voices with information that Willow couldn't have possibly known. She did seances for the Native Americans (Which is certainly something I've never heard of before). And she practiced Wiccan arts." I tried to scroll through my phone with frozen fingers to show him proof.

Adam scoffed at me. "She wasn't a damned witch."

"Look at this landscape she bainted," I exclaimed with my entire face, since, after one minute outside, my mouth, chin, nose, and forehead were already melded together as one single, frozen, facial entity. Adam glanced at the painting on my phone as we walked. "Look at these trees," I said, "and you'll see they're completely out of brobortion to the ac-shall location she bainted!" (My frozen mouth could only speak like a ventriloquist's now, with limited to no movement.)

"So?"

"So it doesn't wake sense! She wouldn't do that! Now look at these wictures of that same landscape, vorty-vour years later. It now looks exactly like she wainted it! She could see the wuture, and that's why she left wehind those sculwtures for Dutton! She knew he'd be in trouwle without her, and she wanted to helw him out!"

From under his woolly scarf, Adam's diction came out perfectly through the grey, after-dusk nip. "Oh right. So because Willow was some legendary artist who painted bloody motifs, now Dutton was either selling her old, blood-soaked sculptures, or else he murdered her, and now she 'is' the art. You told me all of your conspiracy theories before."

We came to the door of the Carleton gallery and I stopped him before he went in. "It's totally wossiwle! Her wody was never vound! Waywe he killed her, and she's *in his sculwtures!* With others!" My numbed mouthface's movement was now more like that of the ventriloquist's dummy. Jaw only.

Adam looked at me in disbelief, but it was obvious to me that this thought had also occurred to him. He opened the door, and we entered the warm, toasty gallery, doffing our hats and shaking snow off our boots. Adam made a beeline to his science friend who was standing in a gathering off to the side in front of a table of plastic cups filled with white wine. Dozens of well-dressed students and faculty milled around at what the sign stated was the "Art Majors' Exhibit," while someone gave an informal speech. Adam grabbed a cup of wine, and he and his science friend spoke to each other in not-so-quiet tones.

I looked around and saw the college's Willow James painting on the other side of the gallery, the one entitled *All of Me*, displayed with a spotlight illuminating its bright, flaming, surreal, body-like images. Checking to see no one was looking, I walked over to admire it.

Then, just as I made to leave, I dug my fingernail softly into the whirling images, leaving a barely noticeable indentation in the paint, and quickly walked out through the heavily pressurized, tinted glass door which self-slammed behind me as I hurried back out into the elements, jamming my fat noggin into my pussy hat again (I felt a little like Jesse James).

No one saw me, and no one knew that I had another item for my growing collection.

Adam

"Did you hear about Boss Hog?"

I looked at young Josh Larkin like he'd lost his ever-flipping mind. "I beg your pardon?"

"Y'know, the Sheriff of Nottingham, *Der Kommissar*," explained Larkin, "That stereotypical, fruitcake-y, grizzled, old, curmudgeonly Northfield cop—Jesus, could that painting look more like a vagina?"

"Yeah, Sheriff Janssen," I said, connecting the dots. "What about him?"

"He's busted," said Larkin, chewing crackers and cheese with his mouth open. I waited for any kind of elaboration from the ultimate frisbee-playing, twenty-eight-year-old nutty professor, but none came.

"*Well?* What do you mean? *What happened?*" I asked.

"He's in jail!" Larkin said, beaming and holding up his smartphone. "For good! Breaking news! Just now! The arraignment's over! They're holding Northfield's Joe Friday without bail in Minneapolis! He's busted!"

I shook my head in stupefaction, as if trying to jar something loose, saying, "I knew he'd already been in custody for the past week, but...wow!"

"That's what happens when you've captured the

attention of the news media, baby," Joshua claimed as he poured an entire cup of wine down his throat, seemingly without ever swallowing. "Everything gets expedited. Dutton's dad, Dan-whatever, *turned on the sheriff*, and now Commissioner Gordon is going down!"

"Could we have some quiet over there please?" said an art teacher to Joshua and me. I quickly separated from Larkin, not wanting to be drawn into his poisonous, troublemaking, young aura because my mind was currently *reeling*. Looking around to ask Emma if she had heard this news, I couldn't find her anywhere. Perhaps I was a bit brusque with her (I'd apologize later), but events had been unfolding recently that were leaving me dumbfounded, especially after the sheriff and Dan Auerbach were brought in by the FBI for questioning over the deaths of four people!

The FBI had found the remains of two adults and two children, from what they estimated was around forty years ago.

I leaned against a wall, out of view of the wine-and-cheese gathering (Josh and I attended most of them. We did need sustenance, after all), and I took out my old cracked phone so I could get caught up on this latest news. Supposedly, according to the hopefully-real articles I was scrolling through on Facebook, Dan Auerbach had spilled the beans to the FBI regarding the whole mystery surrounding the James Family.

According to Buzzfeed, it started when the Jameses decided to move to Minnesota, expressing interest in a building for lease which was then a small, Native American trading post whose owners were having financial difficulties. The owners (the Lindens, a family of four) didn't want to leave and were creating problems with the reservation and the surrounding towns.

Then a mysterious fire burnt down the entire rear half of the building, and the Linden family disappeared.

Now, forty years later (according to yahoo! News), Daniel Auerbach had told the FBI that he personally ordered that fire to be set.

And the arson was perpetrated by none other than Northfield, Minnesota Sheriff, Julius Janssen.

Obviously, the national news grabbed on to the scandal and sensationalized every breaking morsel of info with trumped-up, brightly scrolling chyrons and headlines, flooding social media with basically some variation of "Arson Homicide by Police" or "FBI Uncovers More Skeletons Buried at James Art Studio." *So now*, amongst still-frequent comparisons between Dutton James and Jeffrey Dahmer, the remains of four *more* humans beings had been found from a fire that was started almost forty years ago.

And this was why Sheriff Julius Janssen was being tried for quadruple homicide.

The people at the Art Majors' exhibit began applauding. Evidently the speeches were over. I joined the group, but what I was really enthusiastically clapping for was the rule of law because it seemed to be working at the moment.

Sheriff Janssen was a murderer, and he was going down for it.

Sheriff Janssen

Sheriff Julius Merriwether Janssen sat stoically and watched as Samuel Flying Lightfeather pointed his huge finger at him. "I saw you do it! I saw you set the fire!"

Sheriff Janssen's lawyer clasped his hands behind his back. "If you saw my client do it, then why didn't you *say anything* over all these years?"

"I admit that," said Lightfeather from the stand. "I didn't say anything. I took their money. But that was because I didn't know that anybody had *died*. That my friends had perished. I didn't know for sure 'til now that *that fire killed four of my people*. And that man did it. Julius Janssen did it."

"And do you believe—"

"I'm not finished." Lightfeather turned and stared into the sheriff's eyes from the stand. "That was the beginning of the curse. You forced us, with this arson and this murder, to let your white people move on to our sacred grounds."

"Mr. Lightfeather," retorted the lawyer. "First of all, please do not address my client, and secondly, no one 'forced' you to do anything. As you just stated, you sold out and accepted money, didn't you? And you've continued to accept money for that decision of yours all the way up until last month, didn't you?"

"And now," Lightfeather continued, "underneath the building that the sheriff and Dan Auerbach were *preventing the FBI from investigating*, now they find the dead bodies of my friends that Dan Auerbach and Julius Janssen burned and buried..."

"Your honor, I object!"

"Objection sustained," said the judge. "Mr. Lightfeather, you will refrain from making judgements on who buried anything forty years ago." She banged her gavel. "We are in recess until tomorrow morning at nine a.m. when we will continue with Mr. Lightfeather's testimony. Dismissed." She banged the gavel again.

As he was leaving the courtroom, Lightfeather leered at Dan Auerbach, who was sitting in the court's gallery beside Maya Slotky. *"Hey Dan!* Heard you had an Indian family killed so your wife could acquire some *tin-shanty art studio."* Lightfeather stared at Dan threateningly. "Maybe you better *watch your back."*

The sheriff gazed around in disbelief as he was led out of the courtroom to be transferred back to his filthy jail cell, the ultimate injustice for a man who so steadfastly served the public for lo, these many years. The sheriff appeared frustrated that he wasn't able to testify until the following day (when he would produce evidence to nail that bastard, Dan Auerbach, to the cross).

Sheriff Julius smirked as he was loaded on to the

transportation van and handcuffed alongside six or seven hard-case criminals, half of them who looked like murderous, drunken Indians. The ignominy of this irony was not lost on the sheriff.

The van's door slammed shut, and the sheriff leaned against the van's wall, trying to achieve a modicum of comfort, and as soon as the van started moving out, one of those murderous, drunken Indians, the one sitting next to him, produced a stone shiv and slit the throat of Sheriff Julius, rendering him soundless, while the Indian sitting on the other side of him stabbed him in the stomach, repeatedly (twenty-three times, the official report said), with another stone shiv that resembled a large arrowhead.

Sheriff Janssen slumped down, gurgling from his severed throat through a pulsing geyser of blood, likely hoping, with his last mortal thought, that this would be the lead story on the news that night, and wondering how they would sum up his impressive, highly decorated career as the long-time sheriff of the town that once brought down the notorious Jesse James.

But if he *had* thought this, he would have been mistaken. His death didn't lead the news that night.

The lead story concerned the discovery by FBI scientists on how, exactly, Dutton James' sculptures had been created. Because it turned out it wasn't art developed in the typical way.

It was now revealed that what the late Sheriff Julius Janssen had previously assumed about Dutton

James was incorrect. It was the same assumption made by both Emma Kincaide and Adam Winters, and they were wrong too. Because it had now been discovered that Dutton James had not actually been digging in the ground to hide his sculptures.

He was digging the sculptures up from the earth.

He didn't create them.

He discovered them.

Dutton James' sculptures were, in truth, random objects a brain-damaged man-child dug up from the dirt, underneath what used to be known as the Willow James Art Studio.

And now it had also been discovered that those objects, Dutton's "sculptures," were shapes that had been unintentionally disfigured underground by hundreds of gallons of spilt art chemicals and paint-thinning acids, after previously being distorted and forged by the fury of fire.

Dutton's "sculptures" were now factually known to be, in reality, dozens, maybe hundreds, of the grotesquely calcified remains of ancient, deceased Native American people, buried in the soil below.

What the Native American protestors were saying was the truth: Dutton, and now the FBI, had been digging on the outer perimeter of a sacred, Indian territory. And Dutton James had been digging up the remains of ancient Native American people and selling them as art.

The FBI reported that the steel building had been placed on top of what appeared to be a mass grave on the outskirts of forgotten burial land (assumed to be filled with the bodies of outlaws and enemies of the ancient Sioux and Dakota tribes, considering the lack of appropriate rituals displayed in the method of interment).

Most of the remains were found to be from around a century ago, give or take, except for the bodies found on the very top of the mass grave of buried human remains.

On the top of the heap, there was DNA found with four specific identities, and they were newer. The remains were from around forty years ago. They were identified as that of the building's previous occupants, the Linden family, former owners of Johnny Linden's Trading Post.

The Lindens' bodies, however, mostly weren't there. Because, seeing as they were located at the peak of the pile, it turned out the Linden family had been the first of Dutton's "sculptures."

Sure enough, when the FBI tested the "sculptures" which were sold in December's New York auction, more than a dozen of them contained at least some DNA of the four members of the Linden family.

And Dutton's masterpiece, the gargantuan, encased, gorgon-like form known as Dutton James' *"Demon Lady"*? That was Johnny Linden, himself. Johnny Linden was a tall man, like Samuel Lightfeather who was six-two, but Johnny was much taller, more like six-foot, six-inches. And at the moment, Johnny Linden was on display at the London Museum of Art.

The sheriff's death was only fitting, if only because he was the one who fired the first shot. He was the one who activated what was widely known as the James Family Curse when he made the unfortunate decision to set fire to Johnny Linden's Trading Post in 1981. Because in doing this, he not only incinerated a Native American family of four from the Sopee-Sioux tribe, but he caused a chain-reaction underground, fusing together scores of subterranean cadavers with the cauterization of fire, followed by an art studio that leaked toxic acids over and through them, unknowingly distorting and transfiguring bones and sinews with acids, in essence allowing the remains to bloom in the earth in the forms of gruesome, exploding flowers encased in chemical shells, and in effect, putting the finishing touches on Dutton's wares that he would eventually dig up from the ground and, along with his father, peddle to the world as new, sensational, groundbreaking art.

And that was how the late Dutton James got to live his American dream.

Dan Auerbach

The court reporter is speaking to the bailiff in soft, morose tones, noted The Silver Jackal, Dan Auerbach that next day.

At nine a.m., the judge entered somberly, sat down, and sighed.

"As many of you know," she began, "the defendant in this trial, Sheriff Julius Janssen, was killed after he left court last evening."

The standing-room-only court gallery, consisting mostly of reporters and lovers/haters of the James Family, stayed mostly silent, other than a few whispers. Everybody obviously knew this information. After the fourteen-straight-hour Night and Morning News media blitz picked up on it (officially seven p.m. to nine a.m., concluding at the end of *Morning Joe*), it had been trumpeting out *ad nauseam*. This news was already so-yesterday.

So far, so good, thought the judge and continued aloud: "Because of this, we will be suspending this trial..."

All at once there were loud shouts and buzz from the gallery, mixed with a 1,000-plus decibel clicking of cameras.

"...seeing as the defendant is deceased, and there is no defendant left to try."

Shouting and buzzing and clicking.

"*Silence in the court!*" bellowed the judge, banging her gavel. "Or I will remove everyone from the gallery, am I understood?"

The buzzing, shouting, and clicking sputtered to a halt.

"At the very least, I will remove all the cameras and force you to take pictures with your cell phones!" barked Judge Maxine Rivers-Dilsey at the misbehaving throng. "Why do you still have those loud cameras anyway?! A camera phone is silent when used properly, and they take great pictures! You can zoom in! You can use filters! Like sepia! Why do we still have the loud-clicking cameras?"

Silence.

"In this digital age of ours?"

Equal silence.

"In addition to this," continued the judge, slowly testing her naughty audience, "even though it has no bearing on this case, I feel I should also inform you that I have just received news that the assailants who killed Sheriff Janssen have both been found dead in their holding cells this morning."

A stunned charge swept through the courtroom!

"This court was consulted on whether this was pertinent information relating to our trial, and I ruled that it wasn't, and the news could be released to the press."

All of a sudden, everyone's phones exploded simultaneously like pinball machines with this news, and all attention transferred from Judge Rivers-Dilsey to their own devices. The judge continued loudly over the contrasting marimba beats: "This would account for your cell phones lighting up like Christmas trees right now and turning my courtroom into a Jamaican Yuletide with all those damn steel-drum ringtones. All of which is especially ironic since all of these phones are supposed to be turned *OFF!*" Judge Maxine banged her gavel loudly over her last, shouted word, and the majority of the gallery hurriedly toggled their phone's volume switches to mute (for real this time), or just roughly shoved them into their pockets in a desperate attempt to drown out their stupid, incessantly buzzing, light-up appendage thingy which *used* to be called a telephone (odd, since when they dropped the "tele" off "telephone," the new version, simply called the "phone" without the "tele," was more like a *tele*-vision than the old *tele*-phone ever was).

"Is my courtroom a Turks and Caicos Yuletide-screening of the Jamaican bobsled movie *Cool Runnings*, Mr. Cuttesan?"

George Cuttesan of the *Minneapolis Tribune* looked down at the floor with obvious contrition and admitted, "No, it is not."

"So..." continued the judge (staring down at Cuttesan and daring him like Medusa the Gorgon to look up at her), "...despite this newly breaking news of Mr. Janssen's assailants' "*apparent* suicide by hanging" which has no relevance to this case—"

A shout from the gallery: *"Those were suicide-bombers, Indian-style, brothers!"* It was Samuel Lightfeather, who was already being removed from the courtroom by two quick-acting policeman, placed just so at the back of the gallery in order to confiscate this type of outburst from public sight. *"Solidarity, my Native American brothers!"* shouted Samuel Flying Lightfeather as he was dragged out the door, with his black hat somehow flying upwards to the ceiling when it was inadvertently smacked in the scuffle.

"So, in light of the untimely demise of Sheriff Julius Janssen, and in light of the fact that one of the guilty parties..." Judge Maxine glared at Dan Auerbach in the gallery, "...was granted the opportunity to turn states' evidence and receive a sweetheart deal of immunity from sentencing in this case, simply because they were the first one to tattle on the other..." She continued to glare poniards at Dan, "...and even though Mr. Auerbach didn't light the match that killed those four people—that was Sheriff Julius Janssen who did that—still, Mr. Auerbach ordered it to be done... *Irregardless* of all these disturbing facts, it seems that once again the rich guy with all the expensive lawyers is able to outwait and out-white the system. So I am prepared to rule this nasty trial over and done with." The judge waited for her own outburst's expected reaction to subside, tapping the gavel and coaxing them. "That's enough..."

Then Judge Maxine Rivers-Dilsey did something that was surprising to even the most cynical journalist. Because this judge had decided, about fifteen minutes ago, that today she was going to become one of those *go-viral judges* and have her turn in the spotlight (Not that she would ever admit to it in twenty lifetimes. Still. She was doing it). After this, Judge Rivers-Dilsey would forever be synonymous with those judicial legends who famously teared up during their verbal summations, effectively whisking away the Jury Foremans' already-fleeting-fifteen-seconds-of-fame, mere moments after the spotlight had begun to warm their faces.

All the same, *this* judge had decided she was going to go for judicial notoriety. Right now. This was to be her YouTube moment. So, before she dismissed the courtroom, Judge Rivers-Dilsey sat back and stared straight at Dan Auerbach, seated in the gallery, two rows behind the defendant's table.

"I just have to ask you one thing, Mr. Auerbach," said the judge. "Did you know?"

The Silver Jackal sat up a little at the sound of his name and shot a look at the defendant's table. The lawyer sprang to his feet in protest.

"Your honor, this is outrageous! Mr. Auerbach is not even a witness in this case anymore!"

Then Dan Auerbach's silky-smooth voice floated through the chamber (because he *just couldn't leave it alone*). "This is no longer an official case, is that true?"

The judge smiled because she may have hooked something. "Yes, Mr. Auerbach, this is off the official record." The judge turned to the stenographer and told her to stop typing. "Mr. Auerbach, did you previously know that Dutton's art was made from the bodies of dead Native Americans?"

"Your honor, I object to this!"

Dan stared at the judge and then smiled. *Yeah I knew*, is what Dan thought to himself. Of course, what Dan said out loud was more like, "Your honor, I had no idea how Dutton produced his art."

The judge scrutinized Dan with doubtful eyes. "Really?"

"Of course not," Dan lied, legally, seeing as he'd never been sworn in anyway to this post-trial, public kangaroo court that Judge Wacko was launching. *What the hell*," thought Dan. *You couldn't pay for publicity like this.*

The judge rolled her eyes. "Of course you're going to *say* that..."

The prosecuting attorney then rose to his feet. "Your honor, even I have to agree, this is highly unusual, accusing a state's witness of, of—"

"Oh, don't have kittens about it," shot back Judge Maxine. "The case is being dismissed! I just wanted to know beforehand *when it was* that Mr. Auerbach was aware he was peddling human corpses as art."

"Let's say, hypothetically, that I did know. So what?" Dan asked, feeling a rush of hubris. "As I said, I didn't know, and let's again get that on the record since you still haven't dismissed anyone or banged your, your gavel... but, OK. *What if I did know?*"

"I beg your pardon?" asked the judge.

Sensing an obvious trap, Dan wisely chose to ditch this line of verbal suicide, instead showing his disdain physically by slouching and waving off the judge in disgust.

"Your honor, again, I object!" said the defense.

"Overruled. I'm going to now bang my gavel and say, 'Case dismissed.'"

The judge banged her gavel for the last time as far as this filthy, gunky case was concerned, and she moved quickly out through the side-door toward her private chambers.

As everyone rose out of their seats, pulsating over the bizarre and ludicrous outcome to this blighted, ill-fated trial, Dan Auerbach was the first one out of the courtroom. Shouldering past a sea of shouting people in the hallway, Dan witnessed Samuel Flying Lightfeather now standing on a bench and yelling: "Sheriff Julius along with Dan Auerbach spilled toxic chemicals in the Earth and drenched my ancestors with them, poisoning them, *and that makes your family's curse WORSE!* Dan Auerbach is guilty, and he and the smiling boy desecrated my people when they dug them up and *sold them for profit! This brings the strongest curse. On you!*" The old Sioux warrior let out a blood-curdling scream of violent-sounding gibberish and pointed his ten crooked fingers at Dan, as if he were pulling out his soul. He then yelled: "I'm going to tell the FBI what I know about you, Dan Auerbach. You *BOTH* killed those four people. I saw the sheriff light the fire, *and Dan Auerbach told him to do it!*"

Dan ignored him like a pro sports figure ignores heckling fans, walking past and staring blankly ahead, but the unruly crowd was jostling Dan ruthlessly as he dodged his way to the exit. At one point he was shoved, and then it felt like someone ripped hair out of his scalp! Immediately, Dan whipped around, his muddled mind half-expecting some crazy Indian to be there performing some voodoo-scalping ritual, but all he saw was a flash of reddish hair vanishing into the crowd. "Animals," he scowled.

Dan Auerbach left the Minneapolis courthouse a free man. As he descended the wide, stone steps, he noticed the roped-off press to the side and, donning his little, round Roger Stone-sunglasses, he made a beeline to them, followed behind by Dan's lawyers, his daughter Lily, and Maya Slotky.

The reporters shouted questions, but Dan, frustrated at cutting himself off mid-thought with the judge earlier, ignored all the howled inquiries. He clearly had a burning, yearning need to publically convey his opinion (similar to the comic book super-villain's desire to "monologue" all of their super-villain plans for public consumption outside of their minions). Dan spoke: "What if I *did* know how Dutton created his masterpieces? I didn't! But either way, what if we did sell it as 'art'? So what? What's the difference between my mentally challenged son unknowingly digging up some underground objects and putting a few chisel marks in them, or, or a painting by his mother, Willow James? I would call them both 'art'! It still creates the same visceral rush, the same proof of life in the viewer! Listen: There are good people on both sides of this fiasco, and I know it, and you know it, and I'm trying to get the nation's attention about something here!" Reporters shouted at Dan, outraged, but he persisted: "Know what I'm listening to in my car right now? Milli Vanilli! I don't give a *crap* if those two male models sang those songs or not! It's the product that matters!" Dan grinned like a jackal and sang: *"Blame it on the rain, yeah-yeah!"* I love it! And everyone *else does* too, and you all *know it!* So I see no reason why Willow's *or* Dutton James' artwork would be diminished by any of these discoveries, and frankly, I only see their worth increasing, maybe even twofold."

The Silver Jackal walked away from the mics...and then had a second thought, diving back in:

"I also want to say that my ex-wife, the deceased Willow James, knowingly or not, *helped create these works of art* along with Dutton." The reporters yelled disapproval. "Willow, for over two decades, experimented with all of those acids and chemicals and the like, so in a way, she co-created them with the rest of the James family. From the grave. There's your goddamned story. That is all."

Dan ducked into the cold wind and walked away a free man.

Maya

Auerbach was always selling, always conning and on the make, thought Maya, smiling behind his shoulder as they padded through the temperature-controlled glass tunnel, looming above the traffic below, and then descending down an escalator to their waiting limo.

He probably saved us tens of millions of dollars with that outburst to the press earlier today, thought Maya happily to herself as she climbed into the car with Dan and Lily, the last living members of the notorious James Family. Once in the limo, Maya knocked on the driver's tinted window: "Drop me off at the airport on the way."

"You're not coming?" asked Dan, surprised.

"No, you can do this yourself, Dan. Just inventory whatever's in the studio. It's all your property, for God's sake."

"Wait a minute. I thought this was your idea to begin with!" insisted Dan.

Maya shrugged. "Wasn't mine."

"Would you two stop arguing?" Lily groaned. "Jesus."

"Well, Maya Slotky, I believe you still have a stake

in anything termed 'the artwork of Dutton James,' and I would assume everything currently in that art studio still qualifies—"

Maya smiled. "Well, that's generous of you, Daniel, especially seeing as the objects formerly known as Dutton's 'art' aren't even *remotely* dropping in value, not even after all this *scandal*. Aren't you worried?" Maya asked Dan.

"About what?"

"Well, that you'll be prosecuted further on," answered Maya, "For example, concerning the art studio fire that killed those people..."

"I have full immunity by giving them the sheriff on a platter," declared Dan, "and there is no *proof* that I told anyone to do anything *anyway*, since the sheriff is now dead, and well, you know what they say about dead men telling tales..."

"OK... What about being sued for fraud by misrepresenting Dutton's art?" Maya asked.

"It's still precisely the same God-made, God-like object they purchased! I mean, what is art, anyway?"

"Good one," mumbled Lily, rolling her eyes and looking out her window.

"Make no mistake," Dan continued, "I am forever free from future prosecution because Sheriff Julius Janssen died before he could say that I ordered him to do anything. And it's a lie anyway because I never told that stupid cop to light a fire! I told him to get those trading post tenants out of there! That's it! I mean, why the hell was he burning down our future art studio anyway? I didn't tell him to do that, and neither did Willow!"

Maya looked at Dan suspiciously. "Why did you two want that old metal building so badly anyway? What's the big deal?"

Dan shrugged. "Willow mentioned once she wanted it to be her art studio. That's all I needed to know. She didn't talk much back then. She was pretty medicated. So I told the sheriff to make it happen!"

"So Mom never knew you two started that fire?" asked Lily.

"Please. She was practically comatose on those pills when we moved here. Willow wasn't capable of doing anything back then except painting, and that's all we wanted her to keep doing. So I told Julius to get it done. Then, as was that stupid policeman's wont (God rest his soul), he bungled things! Tragically! He burnt up those four people in their own store!"

"I'm at Concourse C," Maya told the driver as they entered the airport. She smiled at Lily. "I told you that you didn't have to come, Lily! Dan's just checking the inventory before the FBI impounds it all, and we need photos to put a claim on everything. Dan doesn't need either of us to do that."

Lily smiled numbly at Maya. "Oh, I don't mind going. I'm getting cabin fever in that damn hotel all day."

"Well, still," retorted Maya. "This was just supposed to be business, and you don't need to be involved. You've been through a lot." Maya grabbed her bag and opened the door. "Great to see you, Lily. Dan, give me a call tomorrow?" Dan nodded as Maya smiled and shut the door.

Dan and Lily arrived at the notorious James Art Studio just after dusk. They noted the FBI was still leaving an all-night lookout, sitting bored behind dark, tinted windows in one of their black, cookie-cutter SUVs with the government plates, parked out back. "Where are your private guards that are usually here?" asked Lily.

"The fewer eyes and ears here for this inventory, the better," said Dan. "I told them to take a break."

FBI Agent John Bailey greeted them with a stiff, quick smile while walking out the studio's front door. "What the hell is he doing here?" asked Dan.

"C'mon in," Bailey said, already hurrying them along. "I think it may even be colder in that damned metal building than out here. Let's get this over with ASAP. I mean, you didn't have to come! I told your assistant we'd send you photos of any more of these unearthed, crystallized corpses, or whatever the hell they are—"

"Yes, pardon us for not believing that," Dan said, waving his hand dismissively at Bailey as if swiping left on him. "I think we'd rather document for ourselves which sculptures we legally own, yet still remain out in plain sight at a shoddily guarded, open crime scene."

"It's interesting you still refer to the subterranean objects as sculptures," observed Bailey, "since—"

Right at that very moment, Special Agent John Bailey's skull exploded before he could finish the sentence, and he fell lifeless to the ground! Lily screamed.

Two full seconds later, a distant gunshot echoed.

"Jesus!" Dan exclaimed, ducking down. *"What the hell! Lily, get down!* Someone's firing at us! From like a mile away!"

Lily was still shrieking, in a state of unmitigated shock, so Dan pulled her down behind a tree and then scrambled back to cover behind a large rock.

"Omigod! *What just happened?!"* Lily screeched. "How the hell do you know where they are?"

"It's the difference between the gun's sound and the bullet arriving," said Dan, peering over a car to get a look. "Whoever is shooting is a long distance away —"

Dan was interrupted by a large, mustached FBI agent from the black SUV, running to them from the side of the studio building and shouting, "Stay down! There's at least one sniper up in the—"

The running agent was cut off as a bullet soundlessly entered his left eye, and his body fell, lifeless, on the spot, skidding forward face-first through the gravel until it came to a rest.

Then a muffled, faraway gunshot arrived lazily with the breeze like a distant, quick crack of thunder.

Immediately after, the closed-circuit camera the Feds had installed above the art studio's front door exploded in a shower of glass. Then another camera, that Dan hadn't even noticed before. *Pop!* The reporting gunshot echoes that followed faded away in the cold.

"Who the hell *is that?*" raved Dan, cowering down.

Lily peeked around the tree that sheltered her. "I can't see—" and then Lily dropped down, motionless, face-first on the ground.

At first, Dan didn't know if Lily was shot or if she fainted since there was no bullet wound visible, so he froze and waited for the sound...

And then there it was, the distant blast of a gun, echoing through the snowy terrain. Horrified, Dan ducked over to help her. "Jesus! Lily!"

Dan was shot, and he dropped hard to the ground. Quickly, he scrambled back up, grabbing his shoulder, and dove into the front door of the studio as another bullet pinged off the door frame.

Eventually, a shadowy figure appeared from around the other side of the building. The dark form slowly surveyed the three bodies lying on the art studio's front lawn and then fumbled for a phone and spoke into it.

"You missed him," said Maya Slotky, cautiously entering Dutton's shop. "Get your ass over here." Maya hung up and shut the door, leaving her in near darkness.

"Dan?" she called out through Dutton's small art shop. "Where are you? I think I've been shot!" Maya made her way to the side door leading to the back of the shop, passing all of Dutton's lifelong possessions, now covered in colored tags with cryptic writing scrawled on them. Maya grabbed an imposing looking tomahawk-spear off a table of dug-up artifacts.

"Is this a dagger which I see before me?" she called. "The handle toward my hand? Come, let me clutch thee."

Maya flung open the door to Dutton's back studio, pointing her spear inside with a fencers' pose while feeling for the light switch. "Dan? Where are you? I need help," Maya intoned weakly.

She flicked on the lights. The empty back studio looked the same as she'd seen before, other than white chalky marks on everything where the FBI had dusted for fingerprints.

And the floor. The floor was very different than before. Because the metal floor had been peeled to the sides in segments like a banana peel, and underneath was an area that had been dug out by the FBI.

Maya smiled and crept forward, her spear prone: "I have thee not, and yet I see thee still. Art thou not, fatal vision, sensible to feeling as to sight? ...or art thou but a dagger of the mind, a false creation, proceeding from the heat-oppressed brain...?"

Maya nearly couldn't breathe as she reacted to the heavenly sight of dozens and dozens of clones of Dutton's priceless "sculptures," still highly valued, many only half-unearthed, at the bottom of the hole in the ground. Maya spoke out into the ether. "OK, Dan, now I understand why you wanted to stockpile these damned frozen-in-time cadaver eggs. There are goddamn metric tons of them!"

Maya eyed the back door leading to Dutton's living quarters and moved cautiously toward it. "I see thee yet, in form as palpable as this which now I draw. And wither'd murder, thus with his stealthy pace, with Tarquin's ravishing strides towards his design moves like a ghost." Maya inched forward, just outside the door, brandishing her spear threateningly in a fencers' *en garde* stance. "Thou sure and firm-set earth, hear not my steps, which way they walk, for fear thy very stones prate of my whereabout."

Maya flung open the back door to Dutton's apartment and immediately ducked under a flash of something which seemed to be hurtling at her head. A large shovel's blade took a sizable chunk out of the door as Dan Auerbach went toppling by Maya, woozily unable to abort his momentum forward after swinging the top-heavy shovel.

"Nice try, Danny-boy," Maya said calmly, pointing her spear at his head as she kicked the shovel aside and stood over his body, now sprawled on the floor, "But ya missed."

"What the hell are you doing here? You were going back to New York!" shouted Dan in intense pain, grabbing his bloody shoulder.

"No, I'm on a plane to New York now. Or at least a body double of me is, wearing a headscarf and slightly tinted reading glasses. She flew first class to LaGuardia with my ticket and one piece of my identification, and soon she will be in my spacious, luxury condo. Subsequently, as proof, she will switch off and on the alarm system when she enters, and then make calls on my cellphone to places I know won't pick up. She won't leave any voice messages."

Suddenly there was a loud *POP* as Dan took a gunshot to the leg. He howled in agony.

"Yikes! Wonder where that came from?" Maya said. She shrugged and continued: "She—or I— will also be texting my friends, saying that I'm back in town but am exhausted, and I'll see them all tomorrow."

Dan was then shot in the hand, accompanied by another *POP*, and he shrieked and bayed like a child cub. "...Then I'll be watching episode four, season two of *Black Mirror* tonight on Netflix, since I had just watched episodes two and three before I left for this winter fricking wonderland. Why the hell is it below-zero in April, Dan? *What the hell is wrong with this place?*"

Another gunshot was heard in the tin-roofed building and Dan was shot in what was his other, "good," shoulder. He screamed, "Ahhh! Jesus!" Why are you—?"

"It obviously isn't *me* shooting you," said Maya, looking around, mock-suspiciously. "I hate guns. Never touched one and never will. And you missed his face! You suck!"

Another voice echoed throughout the building. "Take the present horror from the time which now suits with it. Whilst I threat, he lives. Words to the heat of deeds too cold breath gives."

Then into the room from the shop door stepped Kira Cohn, grasping a Glock, with a deer hunting rifle strapped over her shoulder. "In other words, let's goddamn get this over with and kill him."

"*Macbeth* also. Nicely done," said Maya, actually impressed for real.

"Thanks," said Kira, pointing her gun at Dan.

"Dan, this is Kira," Maya said, introducing them and smiling warmly.

"Good to see you," said Kira, grinning and parroting Dan's patented greeting.

"I knnow herr!" slurred Dan through the pain, resting his head on the ground, trying to conserve energy.

"Yeah. But did you know she was a Green Beret, Dan?" asked Maya, poking him in the leg with her spear, "A sharpshooter in the second Iraq War who can also quote Shakespeare? No, you wouldn't know that, Dan, because you never stop talking about *yourself*. You genuinely don't care about *any other human being in the world except you*, do you, Dan?"

"Where are your vigilantes?" Kira asked Dan. "I was expecting to shoot more guards."

"I called them off tonight," grunted Dan through the searing pain, "so we wouldn't be disturbed."

"Well that was fortuitous," said Kira. "Not for *you*, of course."

Dan winced and leered over at Kira. "You killed my daughter, you goddamn bitch!"

"We told you not to bring her, Dan!" chimed Maya

and Kira in near unison.

"Just get all these cursed sculptures in the car and hurry!" said Maya quickly to Kira.

"What the hell do you want *those* for?" asked Dan. "The FBI will know you stole them! They have photos of everything!"

"Kira and I aren't here though, are we, Dan? Not one camera captured our images, did it? See, this is designed to look like a Native American sniper went loco and shot everyone up, and then people from the reservation 'claimed their ancestors back' by stealing the so-called sculptures. That *is* what these pieces are, aren't they? Their ancestors that your family ended up chemically freezing in time with your toxic negligence on their sacred burial grounds?"

"So how are you going to sell them?" Dan asked. "Any auction house or gallery will know they're stolen!"

"Ever heard of the dark web, Dan?" asked Kira as she gathered up the heavy, egg-like fossils. "These things are selling quite well to the market known as 'The Rich, Perverse One Percent.' They eat it up. And now, because this stuff was notoriously stolen from this crime scene, they'll pay even more. This is *my* payment for all this. It was *my* idea to take them. *Thank* you." Kira bowed.

"True," agreed Maya. "I couldn't care less about this shit because I'm going to be richer than Herod after they transfer all your monies to me, Dan. But first you gotta die."

"What the hell are you talking about?" grimaced Dan.

"I couldn't believe you signed that contract, Dan," said Maya.

"What contract?"

"The gallery house contract, Dan! There's a goddamn clause stating that in the case of the death of Dutton and you, *the gallery takes over possession of all of Dutton's art and receives any of your previous monies from any sales of such items*."

"Bull."

"Clear as day, Danny." Kira huffed and puffed as she carried an armful of desecrated crystal-cadavers out the door.

"Since when are you such a cold-blooded killer?" sneered Dan.

"Well," said Maya, "I guess it started when I had your second wife, Linda killed after she tried to pull off her unheard-of eighty percent gouge on Willow's paintings. I could tell that bitch wasn't going to let up, and that you'd be satisfied at seventy percent, so...there was a girl I knew, Marie, who may have installed a disconnect on the braking system of Linda's car in 1995."

"Jesus," Dan moaned.

"I never knew *Marie* was the one who did that for you," said Kira, calmly coming in for the next load.

"Yes, and then she died from cancer soon afterward. I always chalked that one up as the beginning of the cursed, vile, haunting of my life by the James family."

"What curse? You killed Linda!? *You* started it all!" shouted Dan.

Kira slid a pistol across the floor to Maya. "Here. You might need that since you're holding him with a goddamn spear."

"I don't want that thing," said Maya, kicking it to the side. "I hate those damn things."

"So you said." As Kira exited with another armful of "art," she sternly advised Maya, "Now kill him. Pop your damn cherry, already."

"That's true, Danny," said Maya. "I've only ordered people dead. I've never pulled the trigger like Miss GI Jane over there. Tell me something, Dan: When did you find out? About Dutton's sculptures? When did you know he was finding them underground?"

"I saw it when he started digging up the grounds around the studio after his accident. He was sixteen, and all he'd ever do is dig. I was always afraid he'd find the bodies I had to bury after the sheriff started that goddamn fire..."

"Oh, so that was *you* who disposed of that Indian family," said Maya.

"I had to hide them or everything would be over!" panted Dan. "I couldn't tell the sheriff when I found the burnt bodies because I was afraid *he'd squawk* and file a report or something, so *he never even knew* he killed that Linden family. Then while burying them, I found all these old bones underground so I figured, 'Perfect, what's another few?' After I buried the Lindens under the floor, I looked up, and Dutton was watching me. He's like three years old or something. I think that's how he got the idea. Because then, a decade later, after his accident, he starts digging and digging, emerging with these little weird, sculpture-looking things he dug out of the ground under the studio floors, and I *looked* and...at first I thought he found something of *Willow's!* Because I checked and there's no Sioux or Dakota art like that! It was almost like she buried them, and Dutton found them! Under the house! I mean, *I didn't know!* So he and I put a few chisel marks in them so Dutton would remember to follow the story that they were *his art*."

Kira entered and groaned. "Damn, you're still talking? We gotta go!"

"Just shut the hell up and schlep the goods," snapped Maya. Kira flopped her head to the side and gazed at the ceiling as if she were quietly begging the gods for strength. "We're out in the middle of nowhere! No one can hear us! Just like it was designed!"

Kira silently loaded up another box, and Maya turned back to Dan: "Why didn't you just release them as Willow's art she left behind, then?"

"Because I already did that once already! And I couldn't prove these sculptures were hers. They're nothing like anything she'd ever done before! Look, don't shoot me. Look at me, I'm goddamn bulletproof, but I'm losing a lot of blood, here. C'mon. You don't want to kill me. You can't. I'm Teflon Dan. The Jackal. You can't kill me."

Maya laughed at him. "You were the one who set up this suspicious, damned meeting in the middle of nowhere—"

"I did not! You were the one who called Agent Bailey to come here—"

"Now why the hell would I do that?"

Dan started to reply but was interrupted as an arrow pierced his cheek and stuck into the wall behind him, pinning his head to the wall sideways. *"Aaah! What the hell!?"* shrieked Dan.

A different voice echoed through the studio. "Bulletproof, huh? Maybe some of us aren't using bullets."

Dan tried to look around, panicked, but the left side of his face was stuck flat to the wall. "Is that you, Featherland?"

"It's Lightfeather, you dick. I got a call to come here too, but do you think there's anything that happens out here that I won't see? I heard every damn word you all said."

Kira laughed, crouching behind a bench barricade. "This was supposed to be an attack *by your tribe* on the FBI, and now an *arrow in Dan Auerbach's face?* Thanks! I couldn't have set-designed that better myself!"

"That's fine," came Lightfeather's voice from Dutton's back room. "Cuz I also got a nineteenth-century tomahawk I found in here, and I plan on ripping your damn scalp off your skull, Dan Auerbach, for the death of my six friends!"

"And your dead Indian carcass will look great too, Longfellow! Thanks again for the staging! Now come out, come out, wherever you aaare!" sang Kira.

"Jesus, Kira," Maya snarled with disdain. "just shut the fuck up for once."

Kira flopped her head to the side and peered at the ceiling again, trying patience. Evidently, her method of calming wasn't working this time because Kira sighed twice, heavily, and afterwards her expression revealed that a decision had been made in her mind.

Then Kira took a Luger pistol out of the back of her belted pants and shot Maya Slotky square in the heart.

Maya hit the ground like a rag doll, her head bouncing into a resting position, pointing right at Dan, eyes staring through an inert death mask, while blood pumped out of her chest in rhythmic pulses.

"*Jesus!*" screamed Dan.

"Dammit I was tired of her crap!" exclaimed Kira, unloading herself. "It's been *so goddamn obvious* she's been trying to break up with me for the last year!"

"*Jesus!*" said Dan again.

"What the hell?" said Lightfeather, emerging cautiously with a cocked bow and arrow, frantically peeking in from the doorway.

"What the hell did you do, Mika?!" shouted Dan at Kira. "What is this? *You somehow get the money now?*"

"No! I don't! I don't even know or care about any of your stupid money!" Kira yelled. "I don't care! All I need is to sell a few of these on the dark web, get one or two million, and go live on a goddamn island or—" Just then, Kira was shot through the face with a bullet from the discarded pistol that Maya had been trying to raise up from the floor towards Kira head for the past forty-five seconds.

A bloody dot grew larger in the space between her mouth and nose, and then Kira fell back, with her last recorded deed on earth being a knee-jerk reaction (embedded within her brain by the Green Berets two decades ago), as she unconsciously let off three perfect shots into Maya's head while her dead body fell to the ground. As these shots entered Maya's brain, a nerve reaction caused her finger to twitch, firing two more semi-automatic rounds into Kira's large body (now laying alongside hers), which lightly jiggled like gelatin on the cold, metal floor.

Kira's limp gun hand finally dropped to the ground and her Luger bounced once and laid to rest beside the wounded leg of Dan Auerbach.

"Don't even think about it, Auerbach," warned Samuel Flying Lightfeather while pointing the bow and arrow at Dan's head and creeping toward him menacingly. "We both know what you're thinkin' of doin'. Don't."

Dan knew precisely what this injun was talking about, and it was *then* that he decided to go for it.

Dan dove for the gun, tearing both cheeks off his face as he ripped away from the arrow that bound his head to the wall, and grabbed the gun on the floor.

In a flash, Lightfeather shot Dan straight through the brain with an arrow, just as Dan pulled the trigger.

At the sound of the gun, Samuel Flying Lightfeather fell backwards to the floor, lifeless, as Dan Orestes Auerbach's body slumped limp, gurgling and drowning face-down in a growing pool of his own blood, his head and mouth pinned solidly to the wet, metallic floor by an antique Sioux Indian arrow.

Where is this sight? This quarry cries on havoc. O proud death,

That thou so many princes at a shot
So bloodily hast struck?
The sight is dismal; give order that these bodies
High on a stage be placed to the view.

From William Shakespeare's play, *Hamlet*

CHAPTER 3 (July)

Emma

The morning dew was still dripping off the thick, newly laid grass turf, and my shoes and socks got damp as I walked through The Sopee-Medatantwon Mounds with Adam.

It was alarming how quickly it all came together. But I guess that's what can happen when tens of millions of dollars are suddenly available in a town that not only desperately needed jobs, but also felt a strong need to correct a past wrong. In short, to make things right.

All of twelve million dollars had been put aside to create beautiful gardens and rolling hills of perfect, fluffy grass, with chiseled poplar trees and stunning colors everywhere, emanating from mature, newly planted white oak and green ash and yellow birch and red elm (all chosen because of their indigenous ancestry to Minnesota).

And now it was Friday, the final day of its Opening

Week. And it was beautiful. Also, it was clearly raking in both publicity and loads of money. All proceeds went to the reservation so they could put even more local people to work, building hospital and schools here in Ripo Lake, and at sixteen more reservations around the state. The nearby town of Northfield was experiencing what felt like a resurgence, and was even becoming famous in a sort of a gothic, cool, newfound image. Much of this popularity was as a direct result of all the press coverage from the James Art Murder Scandal, and now, this new memorial was proving a boon. Tourists had already been arriving. Giant busses of them were filling up Northfield's few, tiny hotels to the brim like plump-bottomed waitresses topping off customers at the bottomless-cup Froggy Bottoms River Pub and Lily PADio, ever since the reservation opened what the press had coined, "The Sculpture Graveyard."

And that's what this place was. What Adam and I were walking through now was, essentially, a graveyard of mounted, macabre (albeit beautiful) cadaver friezes. Because the entire, gorgeous grounds was dotted with what were previously known as the "sculptures" of Dutton James. And it was a breathtaking sight when the sun shone through these awesome images of preserved exquisite, organic life...until one realized what was actually inside the "sculpture." Then its pulchritude diminished into more of an Edgar Allan Poe tale, come to life. Like visiting the Falling House of Usher to view Roderick's deceased family, preserved in the walls of their "Newly-Developed, Tourist-Friendly Wreckage!"

The park was definitely presented as an actual, true memorial to the Native Americans buried here though, because all the "sculptures" discovered under the art studio now served as quasi-gravestones featuring the DNA-matched identities of the chemically encased, acid-distorted cadavers written on plaques below. Usually there weren't any names on these memorial graves, only generalizations like "Female, Sioux Tribe, circa 1930s," or "Male Dakota Warrior, from around 1850," since many of Dutton's unearthed discoveries contained multiple, never-charted DNA readings from the distant past.

To me, it sort of felt more like an exhibit I once saw in Manhattan called *The Human Body*, which showed real humans in various stages of deterioration, yet presented it almost heroically. Here, though, the viewer experienced the marvel of viewing unrecognizable, dead warriors and their families entombed in dried acrylics, oils and clear acids, appearing as if they were drops of dye landing in water, exploding outwards and spreading out into ballerina-whirling-tutu-shaped-clouds, then slowly descending down like spiders' legs...like true pieces of art. I suppose, after all, that's what life is. A drop of color in an ocean. I surmised, since I was thinking these "heavy" thoughts in this place, that it was *a real memorial*, here, because *memorials are meant for pondering things like that, right?*

At any rate, I doubted the nickname "Sculpture Graveyard" would ever become official. Although it was certainly easier to say than the actual full name, which was "The Sopee-Medatantwon Sioux (Dakota) Community Memorial Mounds," or even its acronym...

SMS(D)CMM

...which was printed on a sign as you entered the park. At first, I thought it was a bunch of Roman numerals commemorating the date of some legendary Indian battle or something. But I digress...

Most importantly, all of this was spread out over the same property which used to contain two ill-fated businesses: Johnny Linden's Trading Post, and then later, the James Art Studio.

They kept the old, metal building intact as a sort of museum of the macabre. The back rooms preserved the now-infamous "shoot-out" crime scene, complete with chalk-like circles, all situated alongside a tasteful-I-guess plaque describing what happened. The ancient bow, the tomahawk spear, and the guns were all on display too, mounted on a wall (with the original, dried blood seemingly still intact on the arrows!), along with the original FBI ID tags attached. Dutton's little art shop of horrors was left pretty much as-was, including the now-eerie basket of sculpture-pebbles, still sitting beside the cash register.

I walked through the graveyard park with Adam, ogling at what had been accomplished so quickly, and I remarked to him, "This *is amazing*, isn't it?"

"And they're not even done!" he said, impressed

and grinning.

"Obviously," I replied while pointing over at some earth movers in the distance, plowing through acres of adjacent reservation land. They were *already* expanding the tourist sight and constructing a water park! Progress. None of that digging was on tribal burial ground, of course. The portion of the grounds marked off as the old burial grounds was preserved forever as this park we now stood in. "I have to tell you something," I said to Adam.

"Needs a new name. Sioux Park?" suggested Adam.

"No." I said, "That sounds like a Korean lawyer." Adam looked fixedly along with me at the construction in the distance, both of us producing literal thousand-yard stares, not only because of the approximate distance away we were, but also from the tribulations we had been through and seen over the last year. We were still a little raw from all of it.

"Nativeland?" suggested Adam. "Y'know, kind of theme-parked-themed, but also a take on the phrase, Native-land? Like, 'it's my native land'? That's actually not bad... *Oh*, and did you know they're going to have a little curtained-off *movie room* in the old art studio showing a documentary about the James family scandal, and then another one about the Sopee Indian tribe?"

"I have to tell you something," I said again. In truth, I wanted to inform him about Agent John Bailey and me, because we'd never talked about it before.

"They've gotta come up with a new name. 'Nativeland.' It's gotta be 'Native-land.'"

"Blah blah blah. I have something to tell you!" I said yet again.

"OK?"

"Y'know the FBI Agent, John Bailey? The one who was killed?" I asked.

"Yeah?"

"Well, we actually went out on a few dates."

"Oh," said Adam, a little taken aback. "Well, it's not like we were exclusive or anything, I mean—"

"Yeah, I know. Just wanted to tell you."

"Jeez, well, I'm sorry," said Adam, frowning. "That must be awful for you, his dying like that. Really."

I shrugged. "He looked a lot like you. I guess you guys are my 'type'..."

"Agent Bailey did not look like me," laughed Adam.

"Oh, yeah, he did. Except he was young and cute!"

"Did you sleep with him?"

"I don't want to talk about that."

"Now, listen, young miss!" Adam semi-kidded me, pointing a finger in my face (although I could tell it *did* kind of bother him). We stopped under some poplar trees by the building's original backyard and took in the beautiful grounds. I figured this was a good place to continue:

"So anyway, I asked him to do me some, like, FBI-type favors, right? Like running DNA samples for me? And he did?"

"OK...?"

"So... I gave him a lot of samples I'd been collecting. I got a Coke can from Dutton, a hair from his dad..."

"What?"

"...a little piece of Willow from one of her paintings..."

"_What!?_" Adam yelled.

"Just...don't ask," I said. "And..._you._"

"_Me?_ You ran my DNA?"

"Yeah."

"What did you use as a sample?"

"Please. Take your pick," I said. "You have so much stuff just constantly falling off your body, it was hard to choose."

"Well, what did you find out?" he asked. I pulled out a rat's nest of folded papers from my purse, found Adam's test and handed it over, reading it with him over his shoulder.

"You were pretty boring," I told him. "Slavic, Irish, Swedish. Oh, and here it says you're a distant relative to Clyde Barrow. Of Bonnie and Clyde? That's kinda interesting."

"Great. Thanks, I guess."

"Yeah, but _you_ weren't what I wanted to talk about," I said.

"Why does the report have the 'Family Tree' logo on it?" Adam asked. "Bailey didn't do the DNA tests through the FBI?"

"No, he told me he'd get in trouble, so he took all my samples and sent them to 'Family Tree,' and paid for them! Wasn't that just hilariously sweet? Seriously, he was a good guy."

"I guess..."

"Look at this: I took Dutton's DNA test, and he's distantly related to Jesse James!"

Adam was silent. "That's stupid," he finally said.

"I agree."

"Really?" he asked me.

"Yes. Because we had that pebble from Dutton's sculpture DNA-tested too, and that pebble is supposedly related to Jesse James as well." Adam laughed.

"And we did a test on me too," I said, "and it said *I was also* related to Jesse James."

"Oh give me break! These DNA corporations are just making it all up! They're just ripping you off!" spat Adam.

"And they tested Dan Auerbach's DNA too."

"Jesse James?"

"No. But they do say he's related to Billy the Kid."

"So *everybody is an ancestor of an outlaw?!*" laughed Adam.

"I know! Like, everybody *has* to be related to somebody famous!?"

"Like it's not OK to say, 'sorry, schlub, but you're only related to a bunch of ordinary folks?'"

"*So*, I called John Bailey on the phone about this before he, he..."

"Yeah..." said Adam.

"...got his head shot off, and he said it was probably because I handled all the samples, and it threw off the readings. Also, supposedly, they *have* been getting a lot of Jesse James readings. Like always. Over and over. Evidently that guy really got around."

"Evidently so did Billy the Kid and Clyde Barrow," Adam added.

"What are you guys doing here?"

It was ghostly Samuel Flying Lightfeather, materializing lightly behind us, stopping my heart as usual. I said to him, "Samuel, what do you do, walk on freaking clouds? How are you so bleeping quiet? You're giving me a coronary over here."

"My name is Lightfeather," he told me as if speaking to a toddler. "Figure it out."

Samuel smiled a real smile. Samuel and Adam and I had grown close in the aftermath of the shooting because, as Adam put it, "The poison was gone now." Lightfeather was a good guy.

"How are you getting around?" asked Adam.

"I'm doing OK," replied Samuel, laying his hand on his stomach where he was shot by ten weeks ago. "Keeping busy," he said with a smile.

"Yeah, you ain't kidding," I said. "Every time I see you, you're surrounded by tour groups, or park employees, or—"

By now, we had wandered to a less populated corner of the sculpture-graveyard, a wheelchair and handicapped area next to a large, blooming rose garden, away from Lightfeather's entourage. However (as usual), we were soon interrupted, this time by an embarrassed-looking middle-aged man in a bright yellow shirt. "Hi, I'm Mike." He handed Lightfeather

CHAPTER 3 (JULY)

his business card.

"Yeah?"

"Could I conduct some short interviews with all of you? You see, I am writing—"

"Yeah, yeah, wrong answer, I'm busy," said Samuel. "Talk to Lucinda over there and have her look at the calendar."

Managing these awesome grounds looks good on Sam, I noticed. *Samuel smiles more now. And he walks around like he really owns the place. Then again, I guess people say he always did...*

"OK, Sam, tell me something," I said. "What's so special about this location? Why did Willow James even move out here in the first place? And why did she want that *shed for a studio*?"

"I think it's because different parts of Jesse James are buried here."

"Jesse James again," scowled Adam. "And now he's *buried* here too? I don't think so."

Frustrated, I Googled 'Jesse James' grave' and reported to them, "He's buried in Kearney, Missouri, where he was born."

Lightfeather smiled. "At one time, maybe. There was all kinds of grave robbing back then, though. Traveling carnivals that would pay to show Jesse James' head, or rifle or whatnot. But you believe what you want," said Sam as he walked away. "*I think* it's why Willow came here."

"You talking about Jesse James?" asked one of the elderly people in wheelchairs.

"Yeah, Jesse James, yeah," said Adam, showing his omnipresent annoyance at any tourist's mention of "the outlaw Jesse James" because of Adam's charter membership as a stuck-up, lifelong native-of-Northfield-Minnesota and their highfalutin' Cows and Contentment Doo-dah Club. I didn't say any of this out loud, but I thought it. Adam did sometimes get on my nerves with his *Northfield pride*.

"Yes, we *are* talking about Jesse James," I answered the old lady in the wheelchair, as an apology for Adam's curtness. "I did a DNA test and found out that Willow James and Jesse James may be related, but that's probably just..."

"Stupid," said Adam.

"Yeah, I agree!" I defensively concurred with him.

"Really?" asked the old lady in the wheelchair. "Because I did one of those too. A DNA test! And it said *I* was related to Jesse James!" She grinned behind her boat-sized, black senior sunglasses.

Adam rolled his eyes. "Unbelievable..."

"And then we did Dutton's, and he was related to Jesse James too," the old woman added.

"Oh you heard us talking, did you?" asked Adam, nodding at her.

"And then we did Lily's, and it was Jesse James again!" the eccentric woman exclaimed.

"Yeah, that's what we were saying alright," Adam placated the senile woman patiently. "You have really good hearing!"

Wait a minute, I suddenly thought. *Did she just say,*

"Lily"? Because we didn't do a DNA test on her.

"Oh I do *not* have good hearing anymore!" contested the old woman in the wheelchair, as Adam walked away towards some crystallized death memorials immersed in seas of yellow roses.

I looked closer at the lady. She was frail, but uppity and spicy with an untamed mane of grey hair. It was...

I couldn't believe my eyes.

Because it was *her! It was!*

It was Willow James!

The lady in the wheelchair was Willow James! She was much older, but it was her. I was sure of it.

"W-Willow?" I sputtered to her.

"Yes?"

"Is that *you*?"

"Yes?" asked the woman again, taking her huge sunglasses off to reveal blinking, confused eyes.

"Because you said 'Lily.'"

"Yes, this is my daughter, Lily." She motioned at a blonde woman in a wheelchair beside her, asleep with her head down.

"That's Lily James?"

Adam turned around at the sound of Lily's name and said distractedly, "Lily James? Does anybody know how she is?"

"How she is?" barked the old woman all of a sudden. "Five people dead in that shootout, and another two, what? Gravely injured? *She's living, is how she is! The damn shooter missed her brain by a sixteenth of an inch!*" Adam started to speak but was interrupted by another animated burst. "To say *nothing of Dutton's death*, and that half-wit sheriff, *and* the two Native boys who killed *him*! I mean, what the hell's been *going on* around here? Anyway, Lily always took good care of me, so now I'm taking care of her!"

"Yes, I knew Lily from school," said Adam, frowning at the strange woman, then doing a double take when in the process of turning away from her.

Adam's eyes displayed both severe shock and grave concern as he realized *he was looking at Willow James, in the flesh.* Her stark, stoic features had been worn thin by the years, and, sitting hunched in her wheelchair, her posture was like a stunned, curled-up spider, almost resembling her deceased son Dutton's.

"Willow?" asked Adam in astonishment.

"Hello, Adam Winters," said Willow James.

"Emma?" asked Adam. "Did you know that she's—"

"Yes!" I said, my eyes filling with tears.

"But how—" stammered Adam. "Where have you —"

"You never were very good with words, were you, Adam Winters?" she said.

"How are you *here*?" I asked her. "What are you—"

"Everyone thinks you're *dead*!" said Adam, completely stunned.

"Oh, I never died. I just disappeared. Lily always knew where I was." Willow looked at Lily, who was still slumped over in her wheelchair, sleeping. "And I believe Lily's life was spared from our damned family's curse because she had *nothing to do with any of this art business.* Yes. She was spared..." The old woman who called herself Willow James reached over and shook Lily James' shoulder. "Lily? Wake up. I forgot. Did you know we were related to Jesse James?"

Lily James raised her head. She looked groggy, and seemed to move a little slower than a person normally would, and slurred a little when she spoke: "So that's why you moved us to Northfield, Minnesota?" she asked Willow. "The only place on earth that celebrates a victory over Jesse James by reenacting it on their main thoroughfare every year for an entire *week*?"

"I kept hearing his *voice!*" said Willow angrily.

"Who?" I asked.

"Jesse James!" Willow insisted.

"My mother has always been able to...detect voices from 'the other side,'" Lily explained.

"And he kept saying he wanted out!" raved Willow angrily. "Wants out of the ground! Wants to escape! *He told me to buy that stupid shed to be my art studio!* I know it sounds ridiculous! But I'm mentally challenged too, y'know! Not just Dutton! I have to take my meds to control it! To ignore the voices!"

I never knew Willow James before, but she seemed very flustered and erratic to me. I wondered if she had always been this mad and eclectic.

"Actually..." said Samuel Lightfeather, suddenly behind us again, "What she says checks out. Because supposedly Jesse James was buried somewhere under your old studio, Willow. Parts of him anyway. I keep tellin' these two, but they don't believe me. Good to see you again, by the way, Willow. Been awhile."

Willow shouted to the skies. "So your voice has been real this whole time!? *You're such a jerk, Jesse!*"

"What do you mean, you're 'mentally challenged'?" I asked Willow.

"I have autism!" stated Willow. "So did Dutton. Obviously. But I am what is now known as 'on the spectrum.' Nobody knew what the hell that was in the 1940s or even the damn 1980s, so I was left undiagnosed until maybe twenty years ago! Sure made sense though, to finally hear the real reason for all of my antisocial, damn moodiness!"

"Take your meds, Mom," said Lily, handing her some pills and a bottle of water. Willow swallowed them and gulped them down with the water. "She secretly contacted me a few days after she faked her death," Lily told us under her breath, "and I stayed in touch during her hiatus, y'know, helping her out when I could. And I kept her secret. Hopefully you will too. Actually, we were hoping to run into you."

"Who, me?" asked Adam.

"Yeah, you," sighed Willow, screwing the cap back on the bottle and tossing it on the ground beneath her. "We saw you listed as 'Definitely Will Come' to the park here today on Facebook."

"But where have you *been*, Willow?" asked Adam, still looking as mind-boggled as I, "You faked your death? Why?"

"OK, I'll tell you," Willow hiss-whispered, "but

you've all got to stop saying my name 'cuz you're going to blow everything!" (Adam and I apologized and agreed.) "Usually I gotta go into public incognito, with wigs and headscarves and sunglasses like these big ones I got on. But, for some reason after all this death and cleansing that's taken place here recently, I've been wondering if I shouldn't come out of hiding... Ha! *Yeah, I faked my death.* I couldn't take any of that *mishegas*. I had to leave. I once read Virginia Woolf felt like I did, to be truthful, so I staged a suicide like hers."

"My God," I said.

"My ex-husband, Dan agreed to it, and then lied about it for me," said Willow. "He lied about falling asleep on the beach and seeing me drowning, or whatever whatsit he came up with..."

"Where have you been?" I asked.

"At first, Canada. Under an assumed name. Then about twenty years ago, I moved to a house just north of Hibbard." Willow laughed bitterly. "Ha... To be honest, Dan wanted me to stage my death just as much as I did. So my art would rise in value. He even once threatened me to stay gone, or he'd say I was involved with that trading post fire, but I never knew the first thing about that!"

"Well thank God for that," said Adam, "because nobody knows your side of—"

"Adam," Willow interrupted him, "I just wanted to thank you for helping Dutton throughout the years. I can't tell you how much I appreciate it."

"Of course," said Adam. "Is that...why you wanted to talk to me today?"

"No."

"Oh."

"There's another reason I left, Adam."

"Oh?"

"Yeah."

"OK...?" Adam prompted her.

"You and I had already ended things between us, and everything was so sad with Dutton's accident, and your mom's death, that I didn't want to tell you."

"Tell me what?"

"It's difficult to say," sighed Willow.

"Just tell him, Mother," coaxed Lily.

"I was pregnant," Willow said. "When I left."

"Oh?" said Adam.

"Yes," answered Willow. "With your child."

Adam's legs turned rubbery and he fell to his knees. "*What?*" he finally said, his face contorted with shock.

"You were just a kid in high school," said Willow. "You didn't need that. All of my dismal, adult crap. So I left. Then I couldn't go through with the abortion. So I bore a child and raised her until she was two years old. And then I had to give her away."

"You had a *baby*? But—"

"I was mentally ill, Adam. And I was *petrified about this damn curse!* And I could not be a mother to anyone at that time, believe me. So I gave her up to an orphanage. And I'll never forget because the lady who ran it had a funny nickname. Everyone called her 'The Fargo Grandmother,' or just 'Grandma.'"

Willow looked at me when she said this, and it seemed like I lost consciousness for just a second. There was so much information all of a sudden.

I was able to stutter out something like, "I know that place! I live there now! Maybe I knew her! What year was that?"

"1999," said Willow.

My mind spun around and around. "Well then she's around my age! I knew her!"

"Emma, listen," said Willow.

"What was her name?" I said. "Tell me!"

"Emma..."

"What? Tell me!"

"Emma, I'm trying."

"Wait," I said. "None of this makes sense because —"

"Emma," Willow kept saying.

"What?"

"Emma, listen to me."

"OK," I said, trying to calm down.

"Emma," said Willow, locking eyes with me.

"Yes?"

"Emma, I'm your mother," said Willow.

"What? What did you say?" I asked. It was like she was speaking another language or something.

"I said I'm your mother. I always have been and always will be."

"But that's... What? I can't—"

I stepped back to catch my balance, because my head was floating with helium inside.

"Wait a minute," I said, "you're my real..."

"Yes."

"...biological...mother?"

"Yes," said Willow again. "Hello, my love!"

Suddenly Adam threw up on the ground! I think I said something like, "Omigod, are you OK?" but I'm not sure because I was trying to get all this information straight.

"Emma," said Willow.

"Yes?" I said, but I was still trying to understand what she said before.

"Emma, listen to me."

"Yes."

"Emma," she said again, trying to make eye contact.

"Yes," I answered.

"Adam is your father," said Willow.

I thought nothing at first.

I looked at Adam, writhing on the ground, vomiting.

"Obviously that's impossible because I just met him!" I said.

Wait, no, I thought, *that's not the point I was going to —Wait, what is happening?*

"I'm so sorry to have to tell you like this," said Willow. "Both of you."

CHAPTER 3 (JULY)

"But that's wrong!" I said, suddenly absolutely certain that I had this particular fact straight now: "Because when I met Dutton, Adam was—"

No, that's not the point I wanted to make...

Then, suddenly, a massive, double realization struck me when two simultaneous lightbulbs zapped on over two seemingly incongruous things: 1. that Dutton James was my half-brother, and 2. I had had sex with Adam.

I felt faint and nauseated and landed on my knees and vomited.

By this time, Adam was more dry heaving, but he didn't look good.

Adam.

Who was my dad.

I vomited again.

"Goodness!" remarked Willow, frowning. "I'm so sorry about all of this! I didn't realize you'd take this so *badly*." (She didn't understand. Didn't understand what Adam and I knew.)

Adam moved to speak, but only retched more.

Lily tried to intercede and explain, but she didn't understand either: "Willow had an affair with Adam when he was in high school, and she was like fifty..."

"Fifty-seven! Yes! I knew that!" I said to Lily (Lily, who was my sister). I dry-retched again, but this time with a just a *slight hint* of happiness because *now I had a family,* and I was sort of comprehending it for the first time.

Even like this, I was *happy*.

OK, so wait.
Adam.
Is my *father*.
And Willow James.
Is my mother?

Adam

"1999."

When I heard Willow say that year, my mind spun 'round in circles. I understood. Maybe it's because I've always been able to think in numbers, quickly. Or maybe it was because that was the year I graduated from Carleton, Class of '99.

Emma was not comprehending. "Well, then she's my age! I knew her!" Emma said, smiling erratically.

Willow just said, *"Emma."* As in, "Get a grip."

Emma did not understand.

I fell to the ground, suddenly throwing up all over the place, with everything rattling in my head like madmen.

"What was her *name*?" Emma kept insisting with this silly, stupid grin on her face. *"Tell me!"*

And Willow just kept saying. "Emma...Emma," with this calm, blank expression. Finally, Willow gained Emma's attention, because Emma was, no joke, hysterically smiling like a demented hyena. *If this is my daughter*, I thought irrationally, *then why is she so stupid?!*

I suddenly realized (once more but with greater clarity) that I had had sex with Emma, *who is now my daughter*, and I purged what was left in my stomach.

Then that re-re-realization, coupled with my new memory that we had actually done it twice that day, was when I started dry heaving.

"*I am your mother,*" Willow finally said to her like Darth Vader's twin sister or something.

By then, Emma had gone into severe shock. Her face was pale, and she lost balance for a second.

But Emma *still didn't get it* about *us!* She was grinning and stammering, while Willow just kept saying, "Emma," over and over.

"Adam is your father," Willow finally told her, spelling it out to her daughter, Emma.

Emma's face went blank at first. Then it became a grotesque comedy mask, grinning like Nicholson's Joker and sputtering, "Obviously that's impossible because blah blah blah," but she had completely lost it at this point. She was as utterly astounded and dumbfounded as I by these cruel disclosures from this demon lady claiming to be Willow James.

I started repeating a mantra in my head: *We only had sex once*, over and over, but some other voice, some rogue spirit of some dead monk or something, kept saying, *Twice! Twice!* So I altered my mantra to *We only had sex one night*, but it *wasn't* at night. *So then* (and I truly hope no one can empathize with this), a visceral mind's image of myself and my daughter, naked, brought on my last round of dry heaves.

Here, Emma was looking faint and nauseated and fell on her knees, hard, and vomited too.

"Goodness!" said Willow. "I didn't realize you'd take this so badly."

I tried to talk, but it was merely more retching. What I intended to say, in retrospect, involved the phrase, "Why the hell didn't you tell us this sooner?" but probably with lots of other nasty, inappropriate language, so maybe it was just as well I was physically unable to speak.

Lily leaned forward and said to Emma, "Willow had an affair with Adam when he was in high school and she was like fifty..."

And Emma goes, "Fifty-seven! Yes! I knew!" Emma said this to a person who, I was now calculating, was her half-sister, Lily. *Is that right?* I sat on a chair-sized dead-Indian sculpture (I knew that wasn't the PC thing to call it, or even do, but my mind was becoming too taxed to be concerned about trivial, PC twaddle). I was deterred from my meditation when a tiny, incessant, yet life-changing voice began pinging around in my head, uttering, *What were you thinking?* and *You have a daughter!?*

I checked in on reality, hesitantly. There was currently an uncomfortable, new family lull in the conversation, and the deafening silence had caught my attention. Willow tried to break the ice.

"So Adam, it's good to see you again. You look good!" Willow smiled an unorthodox, artist-being-social-smile, but I was at a loss for what to say to Willow James, the mother of my child. Willow suddenly became prickly. "Well, honestly," huffed Willow, looking away. "I didn't know your reactions would be like this!" *Oh my god*, I realized, *She doesn't know what Emma and I know!*

"Omigod," Lily echoed my thoughts out of the blue, her eyes wide, all at once figuring out the reason for Emma's and my extreme reactions. "Did *you* two...?"

I looked away, not able to look in the eye of my...my aunt? Aunt Lily? No. Cousin. No. *Sister-in-law*, Lily. Was that right? Willow and I weren't married so how could Lily be my sister-in-law? Does that make her my sister "outlaw"? My illegal sister? Clearly, I was never good with family member categories, but this was making my brain hurt.

Willow went on, insinuatingly, "I mean, I thought *Emma*, for example, *might be excited to reunite with her mother*, but—"

"Mom," interrupted Lily.

"What?"

"Mother, look at me," said Lily.

Willow peered, befuddled, at Lily who leaned over and whispered (too loudly, in my opinion), "Mom, they were...together." Lily then raised her eyebrows at the confused older woman, displaying the universal look of "they had sex."

Immediately, Willow understood because her entire body jolted in a horrified, eureka-like moment, and she covered her face with her hands. *"Oh no,"* wailed Willow.

"Mom."

"No, noooooo!"

"Mom, look at me," coaxed Lily.

"You *two*!?" Willow asked Emma and me in dread. (*Here* was when I decided I was not going to look up from my gravestone perch ever, ever again, especially to face this particular brand of music. No flipping way.) "*Oh no, nooo...*" wailed Willow again as Lily tried to calm her down.

"Okay, let's just—"

"Oh my God!" exclaimed Willow, sour-faced, raising her hand to her mouth (She threw up in her mouth, is what just happened, so that made our shared reaction on the topic of our own family's incest nearly unanimous (It was sort of adorable in a way...)). "What the hell is going on!?" Willow babbled. "I try to have an important conversation with you two, and it's turning into a goddamned vomitorium! Can I have some water?" she called out.

"Jesus, Mom," said Lily, "I think we should have told them sooner."

This particular thought by Lily intensely inspired my scratchy voice to function. "Yeah," I piped up. "Sooner with the info would have been really great!"

Willow retched into her hand, and some spitty pills dripped onto her lap. "Dammit! Those are the damned pills I just took! Well this is just ridiculous. Let's move over there," she said, pointing to a nearby patch of tall sunflowers intermixed with art-graves. "I think this area is soiled quite enough. Clean up on aisle six, need a hose!" Willow bellowed at a confused

Sam Lightfeather in the distance while she wheeled herself away from the newly unpopular garden area.

"Oh dear..." fretted Lily, retrieving Willow's bottle of water off the ground, and handing it to her as she rolled by.

I stood up, flummoxed. "OK, I'm not sure how I got sitting on this, this gravestone statue, but Emma...?"

My daughter looked up at me, pale as a Pence, and my only thought was, *I am not going to let this moment be awkward because it's too important.* So I grabbed her arm and pulled her aside, out of earshot of these two strange, old, bad-news harpies and said quietly: "OK, listen, I know you may not be able to process this anytime soon. If ever. Me either. But I want to say right now that we have to make a pact."

"A pact?"

"Yes. The pact is that we will never, ever, ever, ever speak or think about what happened that one night. And morning."

"I agree."

"Never."

"Yes."

"Never, ever."

"I agree even more."

"It literally never happened. Fake news."

"What never happened?"

"Exactly."

"Exactly."

"And this is the only time we are ever going to speak of this."

"Agreed."

"Ever."

"Yes."

"Ever, ever."

"I agree even more. Preachin' to the choir," said Emma.

We both studied each other for a second, and I wondered if she was deciding whether to try the "Dad" or "Father" word on me, but then we both turned away in unison, thinking, *Too soon.* It was at this moment when I had my first-ever realization that my child was just like me. We both thought in the same ways. Because she's my blood. You know?

Emma is my blood. My blood daughter.

Then I looked at her and thought, yes, maybe we would never fully get over what happened, but I suddenly felt a lot of pride for my beautiful, smart, artsy, funky daughter. I mean, *she's awesome!* A shred of queasiness poked its head up at this point, but I stuffed it back down.

We joined Willow and Lily again, who were warily attending to that same guy in the yellow shirt.

"Look, I would *love to interview you four*. Any time! Just quick, first-person accounts of the surviving fam —"

"Yes, and who are you?" asked Willow, wrinkling her brow condescendingly.

"Mike. I'm writing a book. I went to Carleton, by the way, class of '86, and I interviewed Dutton quite extensively before he died."

"You interviewed Dutton?" asked Lily.

"Yes, for the Walker Art Center Endowment Magazine. Maybe you've heard of us. It's run by William H. Haverford Forrest—?"

"I think my subscription just expired," deadpanned Willow, "but you can leave me one of those postcards that fall out of your magazines all the time, and I'll re-subscribe.

Wow, I thought. *I'd forgotten how sarcastic Willow was.*

"I've heard of you guys," whispered Emma weakly, sitting in the sun on the clean grass.

"Just give me your business card. Please. This isn't a good time." Willow snatched a card from the Mike-character, and he wandered off again. Willow studied Emma, concerned. "You do realize what I'm saying to you, Emma?"

"What?"

"Well, I'm your mother."

"I... Yeah...?"

"Well, don't you have anything to say?"

"You want a hug?" asked Emma, wearily smiling and shrugging. I looked at Emma's hands. They were shaking.

"Well? *Can* I have a hug?" asked Willow.

Emma frowned all of a sudden. "Why did you leave me? Why did you give me away?"

"I... I just told you, I was, and am, mentally ill..." stammered Willow.

"And evidently, so am *I*!" Emma retorted, "I have...

traces of *spectrum autism too!* It showed in my tests!"

"*Did it, honey?*" asked Willow, "I'm *sorry*."

Emma shrugged again. "I mean when I saw it on the test, I figured it might have been from when I was vaccinated or something—"

"Oh, gimme a break," snapped Willow. "That 'vaccination causes autism' is crap! But with me, it's the spectrum autism I don't mind so much. But the bipolar stuff is a bitch."

"Oh? Good. Bipolar too, huh?" mumbled Emma, gritting her teeth.

"Sure, I got one of those DNA tests too, you know. Way long ago, before they were all the vogue and whatnot. *That's* when I discovered I was related to Jesse James. I'm his *granddaughter. For real!* Amazing, huh?"

"That's not real," Adam said.

"Of course it's real. DNA analysis is used by scientists, dum-dum! Plus, I've always known how I'm related to him: Jesse James had two sons, and one was a lawyer, also called Jesse James, who died in 1951. Well, he had an affair with my mother in 1939. And when she died in childbirth while giving birth to me, my father, Mr. Jesse James Junior, left me at an orphanage who named me Willow James because there were willow leaves in my bassinet, and also because I was bestowed upon them by my biological father, the son of the real Jesse James."

I was beyond astonished. "Really? So you *really are* related to Jessie James? For real?"

"Wait, that actually makes sense," said Emma. "I wonder if all those DNA tests were right after all! They said Willow, Dutton, and I were all related to him. Now I see why. Because we are."

"Yep," said Willow. "And Lily too. I mean, it can't be that much of a shocker; my last name is James after all... But then...I started hearing *Jesse James' damn voice*."

Oh dear, I thought. *That again.* "I beg your pardon?" I asked.

"Look, I wanted this damn property because it's where he said he 'was.' I didn't know a damned thing about the fire or the deaths or the shenanigans that Dan and Sheriff Dildo perpetrated afterwards! I think that cop lit the fire just because he wanted me in Northfield so I could increase the town's stature. He only told me that about 25,000 times. With his lick-spittle grin..."

"Why didn't you tell anybody?" I asked Willow.

"I just lied. I told anybody who asked that I wasn't related to him! It's not something I wanted spread around Northfield, Minnesota, that Jesse James is my grandfather—"

"Not about that. About me being Emma's father."

"Yeah, it seems we should have spoken up sooner..." said Lily, looking awkwardly at the ground.

"Ya think?" Emma asked.

"But *how could you have ever met Adam Winters?!*"

"That's what I don't understand either!" I said with a raspy voice. "What are the odds that you happened to—"

"I lied," said Emma, blushing. "I went to the art fair to see Dutton. I knew he was Willow's son. I read about Dutton in the *Star Tribune*, and it said he was going to be there. So I went...because I've always been...*very drawn* to Willow James..."

"How so?" asked Willow.

"How so? My whole life I've been obsessed with you and your paintings! They inspired me to paint! They feel like... I don't know... They just always felt like 'home' to me. I almost got kicked out of college because, as a prank, my roommates and I tried to borrow your painting from the Chicago Art Institute. Secretly though, I swear I wanted to keep it. You've always had this incredible allure with me! God! I just can't...! I can't believe you're my mother!"

"I actually knew about that incident in Chicago and was mystified by it," said Willow. "All I could think was maybe you found out that I was your mother. So I had them go lenient on you. They called Dan to see if he was going to press charges since the painting was only on loan to the museum. I instructed him to drop the charges and to insist that you not be expelled. That was me, Emma. Your mom. Looking after you. Honey, give me a hug?"

"Why did you *give me away?*" pleaded Emma.

"*I'm sorry.* Just give me a hug, my baby," Willow implored.

"Oh, mom..." Emma sort of melted into Willow's arms and they hugged, both crying. After a while,

Emma let go. "Seriously though, why, *why*, WHY didn't you tell us sooner?"

"Well if you hadn't been such a ho, maybe we would have had a chance to stop you two. Sorry, but there you go," said Willow.

"*What?!*" shouted Emma, wide-eyed.

"Hey. I'm your mother. I can say things like that now. Although I guess it's a tad hypocritical."

"Ya *think?*" asked Emma.

Willow and Emma both looked at me, their faces a mixture of *schadenfreude* and *freudenschade* with maybe a little lust and shame mixed in. It is, to this day, one of the strangest moments of my life. Maybe the Germans had a word for it. *Shamenlust*.

"Did you sleep with that deceased FBI agent, Bailey?" Willow suddenly asked Emma.

"What?" exclaimed Emma, shocked.

"Because you *are* a bit of a ho," added Willow.

"It is kind of true," I said to Emma (but, *I swear, only kiddingly*).

"Shut up! What about *you*?" Emma shouted at me.

"Well, we all know about *him*," Willow said, mock-secretively, out of the side of her mouth. "And, Emma, honey, I need to tell you, you *have* gained some weight since college."

Emma looked aghast and immediately grabbed her chin and neck area. (Like that's what people meant when they said you've gained weight. Women.)

"Thanks a lot! Mom! I am not fat! How would you

know anyway?" demanded Emma.

"Because, my dear, I've been keeping tabs on you through the years. In essence, it seems that we have both been, in different ways, stalking each other. Because that's just what mothers and daughters do."

"You'll learn that soon enough," Lily said with a tight smile.

"OK," said Emma, growing frustrated, "I'm going to quote Will Smith now."

"Oh, please don't," said Willow.

Emma struck a defiant pose and glared at Willow and me: "Parents Just Don't Understand."

Willow looked over at me. "You did this to her."

"Me?"

"Well it wasn't me!"

"This is so fricking weird," said Lily, shaking her head over her new family's first argument.

"That's just what an older sister would say," Emma chided Lily. She was getting comfortable with this. "Do I call you Mother now?"

"Mom's good."

Emma smiled, and that smile was one I'd never seen on her before. It was just a glimmer, but it showed that this was an important, healing moment in her life. This was the "it" that Emma had always been blindly reaching out for through the darkness. And now Emma had finally arrived. Home.

Lightfeather appeared with a six-pack of Gatorade. We thanked him and tried to relax and just take fluids as a family for awhile. We were all experiencing post-traumatic stress in various fashions, whether from a lifetime of adversity, or only based on the last year, or even merely the last few dozen minutes. We spent most of the day wheeling Willow and Lily around the grounds, chiefly endeavoring to cushion our massive shock and just try to allow everything to soak in. Moments of long silence were common. There was definitely no lack of things to talk about, only details too painful or sensitive to air at this early, vulnerable time. After awhile, Emma became more comfortable using the words "Mom" and "Mother," but the exciting new-word smell would probably linger for a long time.

"So, Mom," said Emma later in the day, "what's the deal with you being a Wiccan or a wizard and all-seeing, and predicting the future? I mean, you painted things that didn't even occur until decades later!"

"What the hell are you talking about?" asked Willow.

"In your painting, *Weeping Willows*, you painted the treetops severely shorter than they actually were, and there was some weird little red rooftop in the corner. Photos from that year, however, prove it didn't look like that at all."

"Damn you're an indefatigable little researcher, aren't you?" cackled Willow James.

"What was it about the word 'obsessed' you didn't understand?" Emma asked the demon lady, rhetorically. "So then, decades later, they cut down the damn tops of the trees so the stupid Red Roof Inn hotel people could see the sun set over Bumblecrud, Minnesota..."

"I believe the town's name is Cannon Falls," inserted Willow. "And the answer lies with my now-deceased husband, the goddamned Jackal, and all of his secrets he kept on other people. There always had to be a *quid pro quo* with him. So. He kept my secret that I was living up north if I supplied him with new paintings over the years. So he could announce that he found a stash of them and make a ton of money. So to answer your question, I actually only painted *Weeping Willows* about eleven years ago, but I had to date it as if it was thirty years ago. Ha! Had to paint that one standing in a rainstorm with a big hood over my head so nobody'd recognize me. Ha! You caught us. Good job." Emma smiled and shrugged as Willow continued on, "Dan also knew I was pregnant when I disappeared, and he used that as leverage against me too, otherwise he'd tell Adam the secret about our baby. Then he developed Dutton's little art secret as well after seeing what Dutton was digging up, and he used *that secret against Dutton* to keep him quiet. It's the way he worked. Old-school corruption. Submission through extortion." Willow sighed. "Poor Dutton. He never had a lick of artistic talent, but his father shoved him head-first into all of this poison, trying to use this autistic-art mini-boom as an excuse to explain everything fishy about what he was doing. One should never do that to a child, and there was probably only one way it all could end. And it did."

"Like Salieri and Mozart," said Emma softly, almost whispering.

"Thank you!" agreed Willow. "Dutton was autistic, but he never had 'artism.' *I, however, do*," declared Willow James. "I am a proud autist. And Emily? *You have it too*. I've seen your paintings. And they're stunning."

"Really?" Emma asked her, deeply moved.

"Willow, did you know how Dutton was making his sculptures?" I asked.

"Of course not!" snapped Willow. "And they're not 'sculptures,' and nobody 'made' them! It's what bones do when they mix with those painting chemicals that I used and spilled, recklessly, into the earth. I was stupid then. Shoot, I'd pour a whole barrel of toxic acids onto the steel floor and just watch as it sifted through into the damned ground. Shame on me. And I *was punished*, because I believe my present, crippled condition is a result of those chemicals. I breathed them in all day for decades. There were a lot of crazy chemicals that were legal back then, Sam, and I'm sorry. I'm sorry I was so careless with your land and your people."

"You and I both committed sins," said Sam, abruptly with us again. (No one was surprised by his stealth anymore.) "We both took money from a silver jackal while desecrating and angering the dead beneath us, but the gods spared us. For now. I think, I hope, it's because our motives were basically pure. But all those other crazy white people? I don't know. Maybe they deserved what they got. Listen, you gotta do more readings for me and my people," he cajoled

Willow, and then he smiled at me. "She really does see The Other Side! She really has been talkin' to Jesse James!"

"Oh, shut up!" Willow muttered, scowling up at the sky. She looked down to find us all looking at her. "I wasn't talking to any of you..."

"Listen," Sam said, putting his arm around me. "I know everything that happens around here. *Everything*. I knew that Willow wasn't dead. Because I could sense it in the air and the sky and the wind that she hadn't left this earth yet. See, I'm from here."

"Yeah, well so am I," I said. "Why the hell didn't *I* know anything about it?"

"No-no," scolded Samuel with his finger in the air. "You're a pasty white boy who moved here when you were a kid and then grew up to lose in the state championship."

I hated to admit it, but it still hurt. "Sophomore year was a really tough one for me, Sammy."

"Yeah I guess," mused Samuel. "But I've been here for thousands of years. You feel me?"

We talked more, for hours, the new, dysfunctional small family and our new, tall, tan, Indigenous family counselor, until the sunset colored the memorial park a deep, warm orange. "We should get back," said Lily. "I'm not feeling so well."

"Oh, honey, what is it?" asked Willow.

"Just...the migraines are coming back," said Lily softly, mildly wincing.

"Are you OK, sweetie?" asked Emma, leaning down

and putting her arm around Lily.

"She was shot in her skull just below her brain," said Willow, shaking her head in disgust. "I swear, I don't know how she's alive." Willow began tearing up. "And I just can't tell you how it broke my heart to lose my boy, Dutton, like that. He never even knew I was alive all this time."

The goodbyes stretched on for another half an hour until Lily's headache was too painful. The van from the hospice care had already arrived, and we helped roll Willow and Lily inside and strapped them in.

"See ya, Mom," said Emma, self-consciously.

"I'll see you, Emily."

"Did you name me?" asked Emma.

Willow smiled, teary-eyed and nodded. "After Emily Dickinson. Your full name is Emily Kincaide James. I'll get you your original birth certificate."

"Kincaide is my middle name?" asked Emma, taken aback. "Why?"

Willow shrugged. "I had to think of something. Marge Kincaide was our next-door neighbor in Northfield, and she was such a genuinely happy woman. Dutton and Lily would go over there and play on the Kincaides' trampoline with the other kids, and we watched them from Marge's big wooden deck. I think it was the happiest I've ever been, just seeing what a normal family was like, and playing along with it." Willow smiled tenderly at Emma. "Give me another hug." As Emma hugged her, Willow looked at me.

"Good to see you, Adam Winters. You're looking fit." She winked at me, and for the first time in forever, I recalled having sex with Willow James when I was sixteen years old (I don't want to talk out of school, but as you can probably imagine, she was pretty wild).

The van doors closed shut, obscuring Lily and Willow's smiling faces, and they drove away through the dusk-darkened streets.

When they were gone, I turned to Samuel. "OK. That was all bull-puckey, right? Jesse You-Know-Who isn't buried here. He's in Missouri, right?"

"Pieces of him, maybe," said Lightfeather over his shoulder, walking to his car. "There's all kinds of people buried here. Outlaws, enemies, friends, family, both pale and tan. By the way, I want to apologize for thinking Dutton had something to do with the missing kids from my reservation. Most of those kids attended Crimson Herring-McGuffin Middle School, and there's a lot of runaways from there," said Lightfeather, winking at me and walking away. Sometimes I was impressed by Sam Lightfeather's wise humor.

"Well, according to my phone, *most* of *my ancestor,* Jesse James, *is buried in Missouri,*" shouted Emma, my daughter (Still weird).

Lightfeather turned around and smiled. "Is the truth even *on* anyone's *phone* though?" asked Samuel the Enigma, opening his car door. "Just don't be too proud, being part of his family. Jesse James was a terrorist. He fought for the Confederates during the Civil War. Not a nice guy. I'd be careful if I was you, Emily

James. You have always had his name and blood running through you. Might make you do things you'll regret. Like stealing paintings, or breaking-and-entering, or something else." Samuel smiled a good smile said, "Goodbye." And with that, Lightfeather drove off in his brand-new Cadillac.

"I see he's glued all the old tchotchkes on his new car," Emma said. "Plus some different ones; I don't remember seeing that framed picture of Pete Buttigieg before."

I shook my head in disbelief at Lightfeather's rolling freak-show. "Just a crying shame..." I lamented. "I mean, it's a brand-new Caddy!" We entered Dutton's old art shop with an antique bell ringing over the door. They were busy closing up for the day.

"I think Samuel just wants to show who he is," said Emma, thumbing through some of the Indian Nation tee shirts. "Still too expensive..." she mumbled.

"I don't hot-glue my old record albums on my car so people can see 'who I am' when I drive around!" I said.

"Dad..."

I winced. Then I winced again over the fact that I just winced. "Sorry," was all my brain could verbally summon.

"Still too soon?" asked Emma.

"I guess."

"It's cool."

"I'll get there."

Emma nodded. "Maybe. Holy crud!" she suddenly

blurted, "I'm related to Willow *and* Jesse James. It keeps coming back and freaking me out! So all those DNA tests were correct, you bastard! See? Willow, Dutton, Lily and I all had the same readings!"

"Like I said, those companies have always been very accurate with their findings, and are not fraudulent in any way," I said, correcting the record. Emma smirked at me, so I offered the old politician's chestnut: "Look, I'm not a scientist, but—"

"But you were wrong."

"Yeah, I was wrong," I admitted begrudgingly.

"So wait. If all that testing *makes sense*..." Emma frowned. "What about those sculpture-pebbles Dutton had in that basket? Those pebbles were also Jesse James matches. Because John even tested them in the FBI labs..."

"John?" I asked.

"Bailey."

"Did you sleep with him?"

"Shut up!" said Emma. "Maybe I did!"

"Look," I explained. "I *was* curious about the sex-with-the-FBI-agent thing before, for different reasons, but now I'm your father, young miss."

"Shut up!" Emma said again, and then furiously shook her head, trying to return to her point. "*SO*, if Willow and Lightfeather both say that some of Jesse James was supposedly buried here, under the art studio building...?"

We looked at the basket of pebbles next to the cash register.

"Willow said he wanted to be 'let out,'" remembered Emma.

"Holy crud," I said, the truth slowly dawning on me.

"See that basket of pebbles?" asked Emma.

"Holy crud," I said again. "Dutton let him out!"

"He escaped," Emma agreed.

"Those pebbles..."

"Are my distant relative," whispered Emma, in awe. "Dad?"

"Yeah?"

"That basket of pebbles is Jesse James."

EPILOGUE (August, 13 months later)

Emma

My new sister, Lily James died as a result of complications from surgery related to her gunshot wound, only three weeks after we saw her at the graveyard park.

If you include Dan's second wife, Linda, whom Maya Slotky had killed in 1995 because of a squabble over the split on Willow's art, Lily's passing meant that at least fifteen people had died as a result of the James family moving to Northfield, Minnesota.

Then death struck again, and Willow James died one week later.

I was her last living child, yet I believe Willow James died of a broken heart over the deaths of her other two children, Dutton and Lily.

Who would have guessed though that Willow James would be the one to outlive them all? Then again, she and Lily were relatively innocent in all of this. Yes, they both accepted poisoned money from The Silver Jackal, and so did Samuel Lightfeather, but none of them participated with the sociopathic greed shown by Dan Auerbach or Maya Slotky, or even the late Sheriff Julius Janssen.

In the end, Willow never re-emerged into public life like she hinted she may. However, I still hope and believe she felt absolved in her final days before dying peacefully in her sleep during the Minnesota summer, her favorite season.

Then, six months later, on Christmas Eve, Samuel Flying Lightfeather was shot by police thirteen times until he was dead while on his reservation, in what was called a case of mistaken identity. The suspicion was that the police were getting revenge on the whole of the reservation for killing one of their own, however flawed he may have been, the late Sheriff Julius Janssen. Many wondered if the police also faked the hanging suicides of the sheriff's murderers in jail as well, but as often happens, there was no proof forthcoming. It's one of many things that may never be known.

Lightfeather's demise brought the death count from the James curse to at *least* seventeen; seven Native Americans and ten pale-skins, as if the bloodletting days of the Wild West had never ended.

Understandably, there were a phenomenal amount of funerals happening over those few months, starting with Dutton's in the blizzard. Far too many.

The world's collective shock at finding out that Willow James had been alive all this time, yet also had just died, caused a resurgence of interest in her which brought thousands to her funeral in Massachussetts, and a sharp spike of interest in her works.

Still, even after all this, more than grief, I just feel so incredibly lucky to have met Willow Caroline James and visited her those last few times in her messy little cottage outside of Hibbard, Minnesota. To have discovered that she was my mother, I *still* can't believe it, over a year later.

And guess what? The last estimate I saw showed that Willow James' artwork had risen in value 245 percent! (I know I've been talking about percentages, and money and stuff too much recently, but *I, actually, am making money now also! From my paintings! On my own!* So sorry, but...it's kind of hard not to get sucked in.)

And now, here I am, sitting under overcast, grey skies, selling my paintings in August at the Northfield Art Fair, the place where my life began to so drastically change, two years ago.

[Oh! By the way, Mike, my paintings *are* selling well! OK, yeah, it doesn't hurt that I've gained, like, notoriety for being the daughter of Willow James, and yeah, my name has officially been changed, now and forever, to my real name, 'Emily James', *and I love it, by the way*, but I am receiving close to a *thousand dollars* on some pieces and even getting some interest from galleries and museums! Rock it, baby!! I mean, as you well know, of course, Mike, since the Walker Art Center is one of them! Anyway, thanks for interviewing us. It's excellent publicity.]

[EMMA RETURNS TO HER NARRATIVE]

I know this is going to sound insane, because it did to me when I first heard the idea, but my art studio is now the same one that my mother, Willow James used twenty-three years ago, in the backroom of that old, metal building at Memorial Mounds. *And*, they've also roped off an area of the *new wing* they built at Memorial Mounds, and it's just me, Emily James, daughter of Willow, in my element. Painting, and experimenting (And I never spill any chemicals! Good Lord, no! I use organic materials, (although I guess Dutton partially did too, in a way)). I'm using only the highest-quality, Minnesota-made paints, sometimes even manufactured by Indigenous tribes within the state. But my paintings are selling very nicely (for the first time *ever!*) because, well, it turns out I've got some game in the art world. And I've picked up a little fame too.

(An old man dressed in traditional Sioux Indian garb just walked up to me at the art fair, smiling, and then he walked away. That was kind of weird...)

So, anyway, here I am, sitting at the Northfield Art Fair under overcast skies, remembering when I came

EPILOGUE (AUGUST, 13 MONTHS LATER)

here without a clue and met Dutton and my father for the first time, and I have been furiously hawking my paintings all day. (Another sellout for Emily James! Maybe we can raise the prices again! Woo hoo!)

--And now, *another* very old, strange-looking Native American man, a different one this time, *really tall*, walks up to my booth, grinning bizarrely like the type of scary dude who owns a gun collection but he really shouldn't. He reaches out his paw like Methuselah, and I smile and shake it, feeling the incredible texture of his hand.

"The curse isn't over," says this old-school, throwback, American Indian man (he's very, very tall), and then he lets go of my hand, but he keeps staring at me, smiling like some kind of Cheshire Cat. The guy is giving me the willies, so I spot the sheriff and get her attention:

"Sheriff Mayhew!"

"How ya doin', darlin'? Sellin' anything?"

The tall, eerie Indian man smilingly nods farewell to me and walks away.

"Not too bad!" I yell, raising my cashbox over my head.

"Well, don't wake him!" the sheriff says to me, hushed.

I smile, wink at her, and then look down at my baby.

Willow was right. I had been gaining weight. Because I was pregnant when I met Willow that first time, over a year ago.

And since the whole town already knew the father was "that Handsome FBI Agent John Bailey Whose Life Was Ended So Tragically In That Shootout" (this was practically his new, post-mortem name now), the town of Northfield, Minnesota has now literally taken us in as one of their own; the widowed Emily James and the John Bailey baby. That's when we moved here to Northfield for good.

Me and my baby.

So now, his Grandpa Adam can help watch over him sometimes too.

Adam

A football rolls across the sidewalk as I jog by. So I throw the football across the Carleton College bald spot on the quad, eighty yards in the air, well over the hands of the leaping Josh Larkin, and then the ball bounces grandly much further, and caroms off the tinted windows of the art gallery.

"Damn, Winters. You got a gun! Weren't you like a stud here at one time, or something?" asks Josh.

"See ya, Larkin."

"You gonna be at frisbee today?"

"If it doesn't rain," I call over my shoulder.

Was I a "stud here" Larkin asks? Well, as the Carleton Carl starting QB, my "gun" reaped a whopping nine wins to go along with thirty-one losses so in that way, it would be hard to argue that I was a "stud here" (I even heard the Carleton coach once call me a "wasted scholarship" when he didn't think I was listening). *But then again*, I defiantly argue with absolutely no one in my mind's eye, *My record was forty-two wins and eight losses in high school, and that was "here", too, so, uh, yeah, I guess I was and still am "a stud here," so...y'know...*

Define "here", right?

I jog over to see my daughter, Emily James, in a large, impressive art booth, noting it was the same location her brother Dutton had used over the years.

I miss Dutton. He had his flaws, but I don't think they were his fault. He was a brutally, honest person, and frankly, it was refreshing to have had him in my life.

Emma is pushing her blue stroller back and forth, surrounded by her own paintings, which are growing more adventurous and daring by the month, it seems. She's been showing signs of having caught some kind of a spirit that has made her already-impressive art *bloom even more.* Truly. I mean, her paintings that were on display here, today (before they sold out!), were all phenomenally beautiful. Really. Almost as if they were done by the daughter of Willow James. (!) And we are a team now, by the way. Emily James (her *nom d'arte*; i.e. her official name now—my idea), and me, the manager of her affairs, her father, Adam Winters.

Now. As far as *where all the James family estate money went,* Lily's three children in Wisconsin (who had by now moved in permanently with their father, Lily's ex-husband in Fon du Lac), were the only recipients from Dan's and Dutton's wills, both of them drawn up by Dan Auerbach (obviously). In other words, Lily's teenage children are, unknown to them, insanely rich now, and supposedly that's the way their father wants to keep it: unknown to them. Eighty million dollars went into a trust, and then, when they finish college, Lily's three boys will *rep-*

resent the art of Willow James, a multi-million-dollar business. Maya Slotky, the now-deceased New York gallery owner who master-minded the whole Shoot-out at the Studio, received *nothing*, posthumously, after a Minnesota judge declared her contract with Dan Auerbach null and void due to her trying to murder him, which is illegal in most states, even nowadays. Maya Slotky's surviving 10.1 million dollar nest egg went to her only remaining relative, her father, Mironov Slotky, a ninety-year-old Russian oligarch in Minsk. Reportedly though, the US government *froze* Maya's 10.1 million dollars because of something about seventy years of wrongdoing on her father, Mironov's part (he owned two countries), causing Mr. Slotky to file multiple lawsuits against multiple parties using multiple armies of American lawyers. So. This was what the lifelong sound-and-fury of the great Maya Slotky amounted to: *nyet*, other than most likely being fodder for gossip in the snooty New York circles for over the next decade, and then, forgotten. Like she never existed. "Out, out brief candle!" Frankly, I only met her a few times, and I didn't know her. I heard Kira Cohn, on the other hand, was buried at Arlington Cemetery in DC because I guess she was some kind of legendary badass in a few wars or something.

Because Willow James already knew that Lily's children were getting everything from Dutton and Dan's settlements, Willow named my daughter, Emily Kincaide James, her last surviving child, as the only beneficiary in her will. As a result, Emma received millions of dollars, which she then mostly donated to the Memorial Mounds (as they're know in shortmouth these days), using Willow's money to buy back many more of Dutton's "sculptures" from their purchasers, only at drastically reduced prices (because "it's the right thing to do," she tells them) so that the deceased (not the "art"!) can be returned home to their intended, final resting place in "Nativeland." (No, they haven't changed the park's name to that yet, but I'm still working on it.)

And is the reservation *appreciative* to Emma James for her incredible unselfishness? I'll answer that in five words: The Emily Kincaide James Wing. That's what they're calling the new, indoor museum they built adjacent to Dutton's old shop at The Mounds. And Emily paints there for her fans!

"How's the little baby?" asks Sheriff Mayhew, materializing suddenly over the stroller and peeking in, "He looks just like his poor dad, God rest his soul," whispers Sheriff Mayhew.

"He does, doesn't he?" says Emma, squinting and tilting her head at her baby.

"I never thought so, really," I say, crinkling my nose.

"Well, he's got the Down Syndrome and all, but you can still see Mr. John Bailey right there through his eyes and mouth. And I can see you too, Grandpa!" she says laughingly to me.

"Yeah, I think so too," I say, smiling. (Janice Mahew is definitely an upgrade from her predecessor, and she looks smashing in the uniform to boot.)

Emma knew it was a risk to have the baby. The ultrasounds and tests were showing possible Down Syndrome, and she also knew she would be passing on the James family autism gene.

"Listen," I mention to Sheriff Mayhew, "I've always wanted to tell you how sorry I was about Sheriff Janssen and the way he died—"

Sheriff Mayhew waves it off. "Not another word. He was a beast of a man, and I don't mean that in a very good way. You two, however. You've lost so many good people. John Bailey. Dutton. Lily. Willow. Emma, honey, you no sooner got to meet your family for the first time, when darn near all of them died! I just don't know how to tell you how *sorry I am* about that. I can't *imagine* what that must be like."

Emma smiles, growing teary. "Better to have loved and lost, right?"

Sometimes, I, Adam, also have to shake my head and brood over the considered, many deaths that have come to pass; God, so many deaths. All our friends are practically gone.

And death has hardened me. It's hard to imagine I will ever give my hardened heart fully to anything again, not really.

However, I'm learning that as long as I keep going forward, trying to make money (mountains and glaciers of it), as long as I keep achieving that high, then the lows will never really exist.

Some might say, "If our story is a real-life

'tragedy' (because everyone seems to have ended up dead), then why are the two main people alive at the conclusion? You can't have Romeo and Juliet alive, for example, at the end of *The Tragedy of Romeo and Juliet*."

[By the way, Mike, I was an English Major here at Carleton College, twenty years ago, did you know that? As such, I was thinking you could intersperse quotes from tragedies like *Hamlet* and *Macbeth* throughout the book; and that's actually not a request, it's more of an assignment. *To you*. Because frankly, *I could just make it happen anyway*, since we have final edit in the contract with you and the publishing house, and in a way, you're just writing this book *for us*. Kind of like a ghost writer. Hm?

Because all you've really written is what Emily and I have *chosen* to tell you, in first-person, along with your guesses at what happened to the others, right? Just FYI! I mean, it's *only our point of view!* And guess what? Emily and I are family now! A very SMALL family. Now. So *please*. Emily didn't tell you everything! Like the fact that she willfully entered the picture, trying to get closer to the James family. She sought them out! Now, whether that was also some kind of mysterious, mother-daughter-type thing, some kind of subconscious, magical allure that brought Emily to her mother, or some kind of voodoo curse-thing like the voices Willow supposedly heard that brought her to Northfield, fricking Minnesota, I don't know, but Emily didn't just *happen upon* the James Family by accident. You understand? There's a lot of stuff we haven't told you. Like what if I was instrumental in setting up what is now known as "The Shootout in Ripo Lake"? I'm not saying I *did*, but what if I made a bunch of anonymous calls to the likes of, for example, Agent John Bailey, who I might have told over the phone that I was Auerbach's assistant wanting to set up an inventory evaluation of any new "sculptures" found at the crime scene...

And *what if* (not that I *did*, but *what if*) perhaps, I anonymously called Kira Cohn, the longtime lover of Maya Slotky, and told her that Dan Auerbach was trying to shut them out of any further "sculpture discoveries" by taking a private inventory? And then, *if I did*, which I *didn't*, maybe I would have also put some kind of bug in her ear about how Dutton's sculptures were still selling for millions on the dark web (although I actually *have since heard* that's basically true).

Or *just maybe* during one of the times that Dan Auerbach was trying to extort me, by constantly threatening me to not to "make any waves" or testify in the trial or he would "spill the beans" that Willow and I were off having sex when Dutton got hit by that truck, *"causing severe brain damage to my son",*" and saying he could sue me because of it...just *maybe one of those times*, I considered telling ol' Dan he should know that Maya Slotky is conducting a private inventory of Dutton's "works". ("Friday at seven p.m., right after court, while she's still in town! Did you not even know? Shit! You better have your people call her people.") I *also might have mentioned* to Dan, *very legally*, that if he wanted to confront Maya for any reason, he should probably call off his men guarding the crime scene because, well, fewer witnesses to hear what they would be talking about, right? It's funny, when I told him this, Mr. Auerbach reacted like it was the stupidest of ideas and none of my business. But I knew he'd remove his men. Because everybody squeals eventually, right?

And what about *the possibility* I talked to Sam Lightfeather about this inventory meeting (although I probably didn't have to; the guy knew freaking everything)?

Well?

Even if all of that happened (which it didn't!), *then I* still didn't necessarily *start* the damn shoot-out...but they *were put* in a position where greed could flourish.

And even before that, it certainly could never be *proven* that I studied the logs of prisoner transfers and noticed that two Sopee Indian prisoners were riding along with Sheriff Julius Janssen the day of the trial. At this *present* moment, *it especially couldn't be proven* that I told Mister Samuel Flying Lightfeather about it and offered him two large arrowheads, confiscated from the excavated crime scene, to smuggle into the hands of the sheriff's fellow passengers in the prison transfer van. Because Lightfeather is dead now. And so are Sheriff Janssen's murderers. So. *That's* why there will never be any proof about any of *that*. Period. Now, did the two Indian suicide-stabbers *really kill themselves*, or was it murder-by-suicide in the name of police revenge? And did the sheriff's death-by-stabbing lead to Lightfeather's death-by-police-revenge? Probably, yes, on both counts. Again though, not technically *my* doing. Hypothetically, of course.

And even if I *could* have done all of that, it's not like I could have made any of them pull the triggers, or shoot their arrows, or whatever.

Yeah, breaking news! "Adam's not perfect!" I've got a pretty damn big libido too, for a forty-year-old, and yeah, sometimes I even feel like the creepy old guy, wandering around the art festivals at colleges and so forth, trying to pick up on young women. And yeah, that's how I met Emily. *I tried to pick up on her, OK?*

I even used to be an English teacher here at Carleton College, for a short time, but I got "involved" with some female students, let's just say, and they fired me. *How's that for a secret?* Then, five years later, they deigned to allow me to come back to work in damned administration. I mean, *you think I like it there?*

Oh! And also, *please do remember* that it was *I* who got Willow James pregnant, and then she basically had to *leave her own life!* After which, she then abandoned our daughter, Emily to grow up in foster homes and squalor. So I guess you *could* say I was responsible for all of that too! Maybe *I'm* responsible for *practically everything!*

Maybe it's me who's been the poison in this town!

Maybe it was always *me*, and Dan Auerbach, and Jesse James, and *every single other goddamned person involved in this shitstorm!*

But then, I mean, why stop there? Yeah, my daughter, Emily owns the rights to all of Dutton James' old "discoveries", as they're now called, and she has chosen to donate everything that was Dutton's to the Memorial Mounds park. Some museums still show them though, like the Walker, which changed the artist's credit to "Discovered by Dutton James." There's even a *Museum of Natural History* in Berlin currently exhibiting one of Dutton's "discoveries" as an "aesthetically-preserved fossil of a Sioux warrior", and it was *I, alone* who gave them the green light to do it. What is Art, right?

But, what if, and BELIEVE ME, I'm "just saying," but *what if, tragically,* something were to happen to Lily James' three surviving sons? I mean, God forbid, but Emily James, my daughter, would then be next in line to inherit the eighty million-dollar James family fortune, plus all of the paintings of Willow James (NOT Lily's damn ex-husband!), *IF* anything were to happen to *all three* of Lily James' kids.

But I mean, please. What would be the chances, right? Still though, I'm just saying.

And, I mean, what *is* this book *anyway?* It's all just fake news! The whole goddamn world is just a bunch of unreliable narrators! And it's all bull! All of it! Tales spun by idiots, signifying nothing!

Oh, and, by the way, I don't like the fact that you are videotaping these interviews now. I have not given permission for my image to be used on film in any way, so if you were thinking of adding this to some little "documentary" they show at Memorial Mounds or something, think again. Unless you're talking high five figures.]

[ADAM RETURNS TO HIS NARRATIVE]

So what was I saying? Oh, uh... So some might say, if this is a real-life tragedy, and everyone ends up dead, why are the two main people, Emma and I, alive at the end? You can't have Romeo and Juliet alive at the end of *The Tragedy of Romeo and Juliet*, right?

Well, believe me, Emily James and I have not gotten off unscathed in any of this. In the purest definition of "tragedy," we actually have come away the worst-off of anybody. Our own personal horrors, from this thing called the James Curse, are *unmatched* by *anyone's standards*. Because, like I said, Emily knew having that baby was a risk.

But *I especially* knew having that baby was a risk after Emma told me that, in point of fact, if truth be told, she never slept with Agent John Bailey of the FBI.

And, Emma was also smart enough to tell me that the baby was mine *only after it was born, by the way*.

True, she informed me only when there were no more "decisions to be made" (because after the baby is born, the horse is already out of the barn, so to speak), but I think she primarily didn't tell me about it so that I could first *get to see and love the baby*, and that way we wouldn't ever regret any hasty decisions.

I mean, everybody was calling me "Grandpa" already, so why not keep the secret?

So, yes, Emily James and I have, indeed, experienced the most *literally-tragic, Oedipus-level outcome of anyone* as a result of the James Curse. Because when we grasped that everyone had already christened me "Grandpa," we knew that *this was our foolproof alibi* to cover up our most heinous crime of all.

But, *now*, I mean, *that old curse thing is over. True that*!! After all, Emma and I may be entering The Big Art Scene, but we've learned from the past mistakes of our kin. It's like that Santayana saying...I can't remember it now, but it's about not repeating the past or something...

And on this present day, under the overcast Northfield Art Fair skies, my daughter, Emily James has just sold out her last painting, raising the average price on the day to $910 per piece, just as the rains start coming down. Not too shabby for this early in her career.

Still, it is a new age, we think as Emily and I look down proudly on our one-year-old son, Dalton Bailey James, grasping a pastel piece of chalk and drawing on the sidewalk.

It's going to be a good year.

"*Those who do not remember the past are condemned to repeat it.*" —*Santayana*

"*The rest is silence.*" *[Prince Hamlet dies.]*
-from Shakespeare's play "Hamlet"

Thank you so much for reading this book! Please leave a review or tell someone else about it, and check out my other books! THANK YOU!

Thanks also to Reedsy, as well as my wife Nicky, Michelle Pourakis, *plus* my all-time favorite teacher, the incomparable Allan Ruter, and Anne Davis, who all read an early version and offered me excellent advice.

The Native American reservation described in the novel is fictitious, and an amalgam of many of the reservations spread throughout the State of Minnesota, and is not at all based on any one in particular. All characters are fictitious.

The places in this book, at times, could contain some descriptions of things that existed at any time from the 1980s thru today. I apologize for any details described in the novel which may be inconsistent at the time of reading. -MS

Michael Sandels is the writer of many novels, plays, screenplays, short stories, and his own stand-up comedy. He received a BA in English from Carleton College in 1986 and an MFA from Temple University in 1989. Hailing from Chicago and LA, Mike now lives in Northern New Jersey with his family of six.

His other novels,

2036: The Year Trump Stepped Down! A Horrifying Factual Account!,

It's the End of the Word as We Know It,

Extra Special Sauce,

The Water Salesman,

Two Thumbs Sticking Up!,

...and his children's book, *The Magical,*

ABC Phone Book are available, either now or soon, on Amazon, Kindle, and other stores. This is the *first full-length novel* Mike ever finished or released (so please leave a good review, gentle reader)!

CPSIA information can be obtained
at www.ICGtesting.com
Printed in the USA
FSHW010506070220
66881FS